Confessions

Agent Provocateur

Confessions

A COLLECTION OF
EROTIC FICTION

PAVILION

To agent provocateurs everywhere

First published in Great Britain in 2006 by
PAVILION BOOKS
151 Freston Road, London W10 6TH

An imprint of Anova Books Company Ltd

Publisher: Kate Oldfield
Typesetting and jacket design: Lotte Oldfield
Copyeditor: Stuart Robertson
Proofreader: Lizzy Gray

A CIP catalogue record for this book is available from the British Library.

ISBN 1 86205 7265

Printed and bound by MPG Books Ltd, Bodmin, Cornwall

10 9 8 7 6 5 4 3 2

This book can be ordered direct from the publisher.
Contact the marketing department, but try your bookshop first.

Contents

PREFACE
Joseph Corré and Serena Rees 7

RITUAL
Sareeta Domingo 9

AFRAID OF THE DARK
Angelina Jackson 23

GRAMMAR LESSON
Sharon Black 40

OUR MUTUAL SATISFACTION
Vita Rosen 45

THE LECTURE
S. W. Burgess 59

CONTROL
Miss Daisy 73

BELLADONNA
Rosa Barham 91

YOUR FRIENDS AND NEIGHBOURS
Brett Goldstein 103

THE SECRET
Nicole Mayo 117

PREFACE

Agent Provocateur HQ can often feel like it is seething with conspiratorial stories of sexual adventures – especially when we have feedback from the public. Many have written to tell us, in no guarded detail, what our infamous window displays have inspired them to do. Others have written in, at our invitation, in response to certain themes with which we are preoccupied at the time, hence the rather personal admissions of Mile High exploits (when we opened at Heathrow) and motorbiking fantasies when we did a window display in collaboration with Triumph.

Confessions, therefore, seemed entirely appropriate a title for one of our first collections of erotic fiction. The imaginative new writing that we have chosen here reflects obsessions we have toyed with ourselves in our window exhibitions, such as bondage, threesomes, Sapphic sex and role play.

We trust that you will be entertained, and hopefully inspired.

Joseph Corré and Serena Rees, 2005

RITUAL

I broke the heel because I was rushing. Shit. Doesn't matter, they're not my favourites. I wouldn't waste those on work. And of course wearing them wouldn't be... well, *conducive* to those day-to-day office tasks. In any case, I should know better than to rush. I should know by now that half of it is the anticipation. Yours and mine. The time you've spent, sewing your fantasies into my mind, telling me every detail of how I should...

I mustn't get ahead of myself. Finally, I'm home. I can start.

But first I need to catch my breath – even the sound of the door shutting makes my breathing get shallow and my heartbeat stutter. I'll let it take over just for a minute, the tiny prickles of excitement all over my skin, under my clothes, as it begins. Only a minute though, then I have to get that control back. It's all about the control. If anything you've shown me that.

I take off my coat. It crumples in a heap on the floor next to the door, which I'm still leaning against, one foot on tiptoes, the other solid, remaining arched inside its still-intact heel. Time to move. My back is arched so that it's just my shoulders against the door, my pelvis thrust in towards the room. I feel like you're pulling me towards you with one large hand, firm against the small of my back. Okay, I won't resist. I push with my shoulders and spring away. Towards you.

Now one, then the other, off come the shoes. They're dangling from the tips of two fingers as I pad along, switching on the lamp in the living room. The wood floor is strangely warm and alive under my feet, the way wood can be sometimes. Everything is alive. I'm hungry, but I bypass the kitchen and head towards the bedroom, unbuttoning the jacket of my suit as I go, then reaching around to unzip my skirt. I start quickly, but then I can almost see you, watching me, slow motion, shaking your head. Naughty girl. Not so fast. I stop in the centre of the room and do it slowly. Properly. I take the zip between my fingers and inch it down. The fabric clings to me, but gradually unfurls from around my waist, down past my hips, and falls to the floor. Then the jacket, shrugged with that same deliberation off my shoulders, the silken lining skimming my bare arms, and it joins my skirt. I step out from among the pile of clothes. Free – almost. Just the… intimates. You'd be smiling right now, you said. I can almost see you.

I catch a glimpse of myself in the long, brass-edged mirror in the corner. Something in my memory of what you described makes me stride towards it, so close I can almost see my breath against the glass. Facing my reflection, I undo the clasp and my bra slackens. The straps scuttle down my arms and now it's on the floor too, my breasts swinging ever so slightly with the momentum. The weight of them, unrestrained, it feels good, and the combination of the air against them and the thoughts inside my head makes my nipples go hard. They just skim ever so lightly against their mirror images. I can hear your voice, the low whisper, you telling me every move I should make. I start to feel that dampness in my panties. I'm dirty. Time for a bath.

I light the candle first, the one you gave me. I pick it up to move it to the edge of the bath and the feel of it smooth, wide, solid inside my hand, reminds me of you – of how I think you might feel. What I wouldn't give to *know*... I find my lips part slightly at the thought, but I quickly bite them; rein myself in. I can't start to enjoy myself too much, too soon. And besides, thats not what we are about. Instead, the smoke from the match still spiralling around me I bend over – yes, from the waist – and push the plug into the hole at the bottom of the bath. My shadow dances against the tiled wall in time with the candle flame, and the roundness of my bottom is accentuated in the dark silhouette. I can almost feel your eyes on me.

I twist the taps and soon water starts to flow and steam starts to envelop me. As the tub fills and the water settles, I pour in a generous quantity of bath oil and watch the beads mingle and settle gently on top of the water. I trace my finger in amongst them, creating tiny ripples across the surface. Then I slowly hook my fingers into the sides of my panties and unfurl them down the length of my legs until they are a curled pile of soft white cotton around my ankles. I flick them away with my feet and luxuriate in at last being totally naked with your words swirling inside my mind. I step into the tub, sit down into it and enjoy the sting of hot water against my bottom. I lay my body down into the length of the bath so that my head rests against the edge and my toes tickle the chain leading down to the plug. The water is just shallow enough that my breasts bob out of it, slick with the bath oil. I sway from side to side, letting the water tickle against my still-hard nipples, then duck my head under the water to wet my hair. When I resurface, little droplets begin to trace their way from the strands of my hair down my shoulders and chest, and melt into the warm water.

I don't use a sponge, nothing, just my hands. I start from my toes, working my fingers between each one; they slip in easily with the oily water. I start to work my fingertips down the centres of the soles of my feet, then smooth the palm of my hands over each heel. And then up, down and around my lower calves, one then the other, lifting each of them out of the water and towards me. I have to concentrate not to focus too much on the sensation of the water lapping against my pussy, which spreads open ever so slightly whenever I raise a leg out of the tub. Instead, I allow my fingers to trace small circles at the backs of my knees for a moment, and for a split second it almost feels like your fingers instead of mine. I close my eyes as my hands begin to slip their way up the insides of my thighs. I can't stop myself from spreading my legs open, each foot pressed against the sides of the tub. My hands almost reach the top and so I slow down, I mustn't – I'm inching my fingertips gradually, so slowly upwards, towards…

No. That's not what you said should happen now.

Not yet. I know that. Still, I have to use all my strength to pull my hands around to the outside of my hips. In one long, languid movement I sweep my palms into the dip at either side of my waist, my fingertips tickle along my stomach, flit into the indentation of my belly button, and then I take each of my breasts into my hands, squeezing just for a moment, pushing each upwards as my hands continue their journey, up over my chest to my neck, over my chin which is pointed upwards towards the sky, my head tilted far back, the tips of my fingers brush over my eyelids, squeezed shut, and up, over the top of my head to nothing. I drop them with a sudden splash back into the water at either side of me, and open my eyes with a start.

After a moment, I pull my knees in towards me and rise up out of the water and stand, dripping wet. I catch a glance of myself again, my reflection fuzzy in the condensation of the bathroom mirror. My breasts swollen and peaked with unceasingly hard nipples, rising and falling exaggeratedly with each laboured, steam-filled breath. Again I feel your eyes on me, though you're not here. I look exactly as you said I would, every time. Beautiful. I step out of the bath on to the soft dry mat, soaking it with the water running off my body. To keep my skin moist I take a handful of the bath oil, droplets sneaking in between my fingers, and rub it over my body. My skin shimmering, I walk out of the bathroom without bothering to dry myself, enjoying the sudden cool of the air as the water evaporates.

I put the shoes on first. I have to get used to them, the heel comes to a point so sharp it takes me a moment to find my balance. But the minute I put them on, the feeling of desire is so strong that a small sigh escapes from my lips. The tilt of my walk is different, my bottom becomes taut and my hips sway from side to side with each step. Next, I go to the drawer, right at the back, and pull them out, the ones you gave me. The panties are black, the silken panels at the front matching the shine in the leather of the stilettoes. You don't like thongs, but the portion which stretches over my bottom is sheer, giving a glimpse of flesh and allowing the roundness to peek out at the top of my thighs. Barely a minute passes before once again I feel that dampness settle between my legs. The bra is sheer too, black lace, and cut low so that the darkness around my nipples shows ever so slightly out from the top of the fabric. I pull the straps tight, and each of my breasts stands to attention. Once again, I turn and stride over to the mirror, my reflection striding in turn towards me.

My hair is still damp, and I comb it back off my

face. My eyes are your eyes, they follow every movement of my body in the mirror, drinking in every curve as though the reflection was that of a stranger. I want so badly to rush, to finish, I need to get to you, but I won't allow myself to disappoint you – to disappoint us. I take a breath and very deliberately remove the lid from the tube of lipstick, twisting the bottom until the red stick emerges from its casing. Carefully following the lines of my lips, I smooth the colour on thick and dark. And of course, like you said, no other makeup or adornments – just the perfume. I tilt the bottle, stoppered with my finger, and dab a touch of the fragrance just underneath each ear, a drop on each wrist, and lastly I lift my bra and allow a dot under each breast, their warmth stimulating the scent.

Now is always the only part that's not right. If I could just leave like this, dressed as I am now, then it would be exactly as you described. But I can't. So I stride back over to the door and pick my coat up off the floor. I slip it on over my barely-covered skin, belting it tight around my waist, but leaving the top buttons undone so that it falls open ever so slightly. There. I pick up my keys and unlatch the door, pausing for a moment to make sure my hair is smoothed down, take a deep breath, straighten my back and step out into the hallway.

Ritual

These shoes won't let me walk too fast, but even so I'm careful not to quicken my pace. It's as though I'm walking towards a fire, closer with every step, I can feel the heat spread across my body. After what feels like an eternity, I've finally walked the few blocks and I'm standing outside your door. I press the doorbell and rest a hand in each pocket, tilt my hip to the side and raise my chin. I can see your shadow loom towards the door through the glass, backlit from the muted light behind you. You observe my silhouette for a moment before you open the door. But I know it's right.

'You're early.'

'No I'm not.'

You smile, and step back as I brush past you and inside. You close the door behind me and turn around to face me, an amused smile still playing at your lips. I don't look at you, I just let you watch me as I walk towards your bedroom. You catch up with me, follow so close behind me I can feel your breath against my neck. But your body never makes contact with mine of course. I stand next to the bed. It's dark in here, only the streetlamp outside provides any kind of illumination. You abruptly turn on the overhead light and lean against the doorframe, arms folded.

'Were you a good girl?'

'Yes.'

'Show me.'

Your eyes are locked on to mine, but I don't move. Not yet. I'm supposed to wait. I stand, legs apart, my fingers twisting and untwisting the loose ends of the belt on my coat. Out of the corner of my eye I can see the picture frame lying face down on the bedside table. For a fraction of a second, I hesitate. You speak again.

'I don't believe you. Show me.'

I pull at each end of the belt and the knot pops undone. I let the coat fall open, and you stand up straight, away from the doorframe, and unfold your arms. Your eyes won't let me go, I'm held inside your gaze. I flick the coat off my shoulders and without turning around, I sit down on the edge of the bed and cross one leg slowly over the other, and I stretch out my arms behind me, leaning back. You take two steps towards the bed, until you are only inches from where I'm sitting. You stand over me, look down at me, and the pressure of your eyes forces me to lie back on the bed. I uncross my legs and rest each stiletto-heeled foot against the floor. The angle of my feet, with the heels so high, forces me to arch my back slightly, forcing my breasts up towards you. I rest my hands on my stomach for a moment, and then gradually inch my fingertips towards the edge of my panties. I slip them underneath, and run them along the seams down and under my hips which I lift languidly off the bed, my thigh muscles tensing with the movement. I edge the fabric down over the curve of my bottom, and the material folds itself down at the front, over my pubic bone. They stretch in between my thighs and I push them down until they fall over past my knees and to the floor. I remove one heeled foot, making sure to leave them draped around the other ankle. I spread my legs wider. You don't move and your control is more than I can bear. You don't, you never even try, to touch me. Just your eyes on me. All over me. Aren't you ever afraid that one day I just won't...? No. This is a part of me now. I can't not.

I exhale a long, warm breath and reach both hands behind me to unhook the bra. My nipples are straining against the sheer material. I whip my arms out from under me and shrug out of the bra, which I drop to the floor at the side of the bed. I try not to think about the familiar reading glasses folded neatly at the bedside. Instead, I turn back to you, my stomach rising and falling in deep waves as I lie naked under your gaze.

'Mmmm hmmmm.'

Your voice is low, your jaw is clenching, but you don't move. Not even a fraction. I reach my hand down in between my legs, it's as though your eyes force it there. The minute my fingertips touch my pussy, feel its wetness, I sigh just at the relief of the touch. Finally the touch. I skim along the outside of my opening from bottom to top then back down, until I can't take it anymore, and slip two fingers slowly inside. I let out a groan and tilt my head back, pull my fingers out and back in again slowly slowly, your eyes on me constantly, you're breathing hard but you never move. I move the other hand up, over my breasts, squeezing each nipple tight in between my fingers.

I start to raise my hips off the bed with each movement of my fingers inside my pussy, my mouth open and a small groan following every belaboured breath. I trace my other hand down from my breasts, over my stomach and down to my clit. I slick my wetness over it and start to work small circles around it, all the while the fingers of my other hand are stroking slowly in and out of me and all the while you don't move, but I can feel you, I can feel the heat coming off your body down onto me and your eyes are all over me, my hips are arching towards you then grinding into the soft mattress, again and again uncontrollably, my fingers slip around and around my clit and endlessly into and out of my soaking wet pussy, and I lift my head towards you and stare straight into your eyes as I climax, I cry out, my pussy clenching in around my fingers in slippery waves. I allow them to rest inside me for a moment as I fall back onto the bed, breathless. Your voice breaks the silence.

'Good girl.'

You take a step backwards and I sit up again at the edge of the bed. You're smiling that amused smile.

'Coward.'

I stand up and take a step towards you, close some of the gap between us. For a second you look almost afraid. The smell of sex mingles with my perfume. You breathe me in for a second, your eyes almost closed. Then back to that control.

'You love it. Don't pretend you don't.'

'You don't see anything wrong with this?'

'I don't touch you.'

'I noticed.'

'It's best this way.'

I let out a small laugh, reach down and pull on my coat. I stuff my bra and panties into the pockets and start to walk away.

'I wonder if she'd see it that way.'

'Then let's stop.'

You say this up close, your voice low and warm right against my ear. Just like you did the night when she bustled away to the kitchen with our dishes after the dinner party. Just like you did at her birthday as she unwrapped the present so lovingly chosen by me, the faithful best friend. Just as you did at your five-year-anniversary party. Every time, a little bit more of the fantasy, close up in my ear, slipping through into my brain. That was the part of you I had in me.

So I can't say anything. You walk behind me towards the door.

I'm home again. Leaning against the door. The light on my answering machine is flashing, one new message. I hit play. It's you.

'Are you thinking about me yet…?'

AFRAID OF THE DARK

What's going on? I thought. What's going on, and why does he always have to keep me in the dark? But really I like being kept in the dark.

I know you know this already.

On this occasion though, I did want just a little control. He already knew too much. He had tricky looks: he tricked me into telling him things I didn't want him to know. Usually I like people to not know lots of things about me. It's much nicer when people have to make you up a little bit. If you're not really there, they can fix you in their heads just how they like you, and that way everybody's a lot happier.

I wasn't literally in the dark, I should say. He liked candles, this man; lots of candles stuck all around the room in awkward places. They're nice, I think, candles. They make you look pretty. Soft light makes soft skin, soft eyes. Candlelight bounces off curves and makes them look intentional. I think I must have looked really very pretty and welcoming. He was only in the next room, so it's not as though I was truly worried. I could hear everything, after all. I couldn't move, not properly, and I couldn't quite see through the gap in the doorway, but I could make out reassuring sounds and focus on them, and that made the time pass quickly and almost pleasantly. It's a nice place, his flat. It's very clean and it smells very good; like oranges, and aftershave, and sunshine – so clean you'd think nothing dirty could ever happen there. He's very clean, too, and I like that. I appreciate the gesture.

Shall I tell you what I was wearing? I was quite pleased with it. During the waiting part, other than listening, I thought about things like what I was wearing to distract myself. I heard him talking on the telephone at one point and that gave me a jolt of nerves so fierce I thought I might pee my pants. I really didn't want to spoil my pretty knickers like that, so I chose to focus on them very hard, instead. I knew they might look a little damp to him from the doorway anyhow, just because under my nerves were some jitters and squirms of excitement. I was embarrassed about that, because I wanted to appear aloof, but the way he'd tied my legs I couldn't have closed my thighs by more than an inch. My wrists were wound so tightly above my head that I couldn't have hoped to cover myself with my hands, either. I felt very stretched, and there was a cushion pushed under my bottom which made everything ache just a little more than it would have, but more than that it forced my pussy higher into the air than the rest of me – high up and open, however I moved, and my quiet struggles only served to make me squirmier and wetter than before. I knew that the more I struggled, the more I would soak through the silk panties, and the more the fabric would cling to me and show my every line and contour without him needing to push them aside to stare.

Other than the knickers, I'd gone to the effort of proper stockings, clipping and straightening them earlier that evening with a growing sense of anticipation. I'd put on a sort of basque thing, too; the kind of thing I'd seen him enjoy on other people. Even lying on my back, my breasts felt oddly weightless, so that looking down I could see alabaster curves pushing roundly over the top of the pale oyster satin, a half-circle of rose pink nipple just showing over the cutaway of the basque. I found it exciting despite myself, being laid out as a platter for the man in the next room, and aside from the rising panic and the crashing nerves between my legs I was quite content.

When he finally entered, he was not alone. By now I had heard another voice, softer than his. I'd wondered if it was the same man as before; the gentle-looking blond with the unplaceable accent, but as soon as they came into the room I saw – two steps behind him but looking confident and eager – a naked redhead with even paler breasts than mine.

'This is Jeanne,' he said, and as he whispered in her ear I watched her emerald eyes widen along with her smile, her nipples hardening in front of me. 'Jeanne heard about your problems and she wants to help you with them.'

'What problems?' I asked, before I thought about what I was doing, and winced in sudden pain as Jeanne slapped the inside of my left thigh, harder than anybody has ever slapped me before. Despite myself, I felt my pussy begin to grow hot, tingling more now, and the sensation spread down to my toes, mingling with the stinging pain as adrenaline began to course through my body.

'Sorry, honey,' Jeanne murmured, her eyes glittering as she knelt on the bed inside the V of my open legs. 'You need to have a little less attitude with me. Your friend told me you have trouble doing as you're told, so I'm going to help you to learn.'

I wondered what he'd told her. I'd confessed a lot to this man in the past, some things willingly, others because he had made me, but it had never occurred to me before that he shared these secrets with anyone else. It felt oddly shameful; as though it were not enough that my whole body was spread out for Jeanne to explore – she knew my life intimately, too. Jeanne caught the expression on my face and looked spitefully pleased to have unsettled me.

'Poor honey, did you think you were anything special to him? We laugh about you. You think far too much of yourself – I can see now why he asked me to help him teach you your place.'

Her words were harsh, but sounded silky in her melting French accent. Besides, there was still a glitter in her eyes and I thought that she was as excited as I was by what she might do to me.

Jeanne slid off the bed onto her feet, and walked round to the side of me, all the while examining me with her eyes and then, after a silence, with her hands. She let the tips of her fingers brush over my skin almost affectionately.

'Very beautiful skin you have,' she said. 'Very soft. What a shame you ruin it with these ugly markings,' and she gestured disdainfully at a very small tattoo on the underside of my left arm. I had the little bird etched on in my late teens, in one of the most delicate places to be tattooed. I didn't understand at the time what it was in my character that made me choose to make the occasion even more painful than necessary. Jeanne leaned over and pinched the inked skin hard enough to make my eyes water. 'And as for this,' she added meanly, 'this is another blemish on your body. You should be ashamed to make her so ugly.' My cheeks burned red with shame as I realised with a jolt she was talking about my pussy. I had always been complimented on it in the past and thought of it rather fondly; I hated the idea that someone might find my sex unappealing. My instinct was to close my legs, but of course I was still bound too tightly to hide her from Jeanne's disdainful gaze.

'What do you think? Can we do anything to improve this?' she asked the man. 'Do you think it's worth it?'

Looking at him for reassurance, I saw that he was not willing to offer me even a smile for comfort. 'It can't hurt,' he replied with a smirk, and I worried immediately that it could – and would. Jeanne's fulsome lips spread into a wide grin, and she held her hand out to the man and led him out of the room. I have to admit that at that moment I began to cry a little, feeling suddenly uncertain of the situation and not a little helpless. I heard running water and sloshing, and then they were back. 'You do it,' she ordered him. 'I can't bear to touch her there just now.'

He placed a small bowl on the sheet between my thighs, and began to lather his hands with soap. 'I'm clean!' I cried out, before I could stop myself. 'How dare you? I'm clean!' Jeanne responded with a sharp tug to my right nipple.

'Speak again, sweet – just try it!' she hissed. Hot tears welled again in my eyes, but she had turned her gaze towards the man and began to direct him more forcefully in his ablutions. 'Wash her thighs. That's it! Soap her here for me, and here,' she demanded, and he did so. His hands were gentle on me, massaging my inner thigh in circular movements and gently lathering the soap into my pubic hair.

'Don't be coy!' she snapped, and pushed him aside with obvious frustration. 'Pass me the other things,' she told him.

'What things?' I asked quickly, but even as I did so I saw a flash of silver in the candlelight, and then I felt small cold fingers on my inner thigh, pulling me open, followed by an unmistakable scraping sensation on my skin.

'I suggest you keep still, sweetie,' she said, and I gave up struggling then and watched quietly as she looked between my legs with a sudden expression of concentration and care. I loved her a little in that moment suddenly; all the violence had gone out of her voice, and as her hands began to warm up at the touch of my skin so her features softened and I saw the tip of her tongue at the corner of her mouth; she took her task very seriously indeed. Gradually I felt her move inwards; having shaved me clean where the hair curled at the edges of my inner thighs, I felt her part the very centre of me, pulling the skin taut while she depilated me more and more thoroughly. Patting each area clean as she moved on, I felt the newly bare skin cool and tingling. The silence in the room enveloped the three of us, and the shadow of candlelight flickered on the walls. In the peace of those few moments I felt myself begin to relax, and my pussy begin to ache and pulse with warmth.

But just as I felt myself almost beginning to melt with a kind of burning longing, she was finished, and she slapped my now obviously naked vulva with the back of her hand. 'There!' she announced with some pride. 'Now she looks worth bothering with, don't you agree?'

He mumbled 'Yes…' and for the first time I realised that the man would speak only when she asked him a question. I also realised that he was standing beside her with – despite being fully dressed – a very obvious hard-on pressing at the front of his trousers. Following my gaze, Jeanne looked too, and giggled.

'You liked that, didn't you?' she asked him, and – with no warning – unzipped his trousers and slipped a delicate, pale hand inside. I saw her push his shorts aside and slide her palm expertly around the shaft of his cock, rubbing her fingers over the glistening tip, and then just as abruptly she moved her hand out of his trousers, leaving him looking vulnerable and a little abashed. She moved her fingers back to me and smeared the slippery drops from his cock between my legs. Something deep inside me leapt and contracted at her touch, those few seconds of contact a comfort which she obviously didn't want to allow me for long.

'You're wet already, aren't you?' she sneered at me. 'I think you're jumping the gun a little. I thought you might be beginning to learn how to behave like a lady, and wait your turn, but nothing of the sort.' She began looking restlessly around the room until her gaze fell upon something that made her smile again. 'Get me those,' she ordered the man. 'Now.'

When I saw what she was pointing at, my heart leapt with fright. The beautiful black satin stilettoes I had worn to my 'date', so high they forced my breasts and bottom to thrust up and out as I walked (to the pleasure of most of the men I'd passed on the way here), they now seemed more like instruments of torture than symbols of power and sexuality. I was terrified that she might beat me with them.

But she did no such thing. The man passed the shoes to her as instructed, and to my surprise, and despite the grime of the street on their undersides, she took the heel of one of the shoes in her mouth. His eyes locked to hers, Jeanne drew the heel out slowly, swirling a tongue around the length of it as she did so. It was such a rude movement I thought maybe she might begin to seduce him, and I saw his eyes shine with possibility too, but instead she turned back to me. I felt a sharp, hard nudging between my legs, and her fingers opening me up insolently, and then I screamed out as she carefully and gently pulsed the stiletto heel into my pussy. Again I felt the dive and throb deep inside as my muscles clung to the thin heel buried in me, even as I felt ashamed to take pleasure in such a grubby action. Ignoring my yelps of discomfort, she began to slide the heel in and out of me, staring again deeply between my legs with an endearing focus and fascination, almost as though I were some sort of circus entertainment for her – which in a way, I suppose I was. I began to get used to the awkward sensation mixed with the relief of having something for my aching pussy to cling to, and I did wonder at that point how much pleasure Jeanne was really taking in all of this. Bound and spread-eagled as I was, Jeanne could have done anything she liked to me. She could have crouched over me and forced me to lick her, or ordered the man to fuck me, or even ignored me altogether and left me to squirm while she enjoyed him. Instead, touchingly, she seemed to prefer to explore me, embarrassingly and thoroughly, and I felt somehow grateful for her attention.

Even though it made it more uncomfortable, I soon couldn't stop my hips entirely from beginning to move. Jeanne noticed this and smiled at me.

'What else?' she asked me. 'Can she still be hungry?' With that Jeanne removed the shoe from me and handed it to the man. 'Wash it,' she told him, and he seemed grateful for a reason not to look at me as she left us alone for over a minute. I tried not to be offended: a dirty shoe was good enough for my pussy, but my pussy left the shoe unclean enough to be deemed in need of a scrub. I remembered that Jeanne had sucked the heel herself before she shoved it into me and tried to take comfort in this intimacy. Jeanne reappeared with a small bag and unzipped it at the foot of the bed, taking out a handful of toiletries before finding a large hairbrush, which seemed to please her. Turning to the man, she said airily, 'I don't think she has learned to suffer quietly yet; should I beat her with the bristles or screw her with the handle?'

A slow smile spread across his face. We had played spanking games many times before, but Jeanne was crueller than he had ever been to me, and I hoped he wouldn't let her really hurt me. I was tied fast on my back, my corset at least offering some protection to my breasts. To my dismay, he answered confidently, 'Both, in turn.'

Jeanne really did look pleased with his greedy reply. Her whole face shone with a kind of terrible beauty. 'Unfasten her corset, then,' she said to him, and I was afraid all over again. I didn't want my skin marked and scarred, least not the skin on my breasts, but I was learning that it might be better to keep my fear to myself. The man moved around the bed, the bulge of his eager cock obvious and garish in his shorts through his gaping jeans, and began to unhook the front of my corset. I shut my eyes, refusing to look into his as he betrayed me. We had never agreed on this. There was always a limit, in the past; an unspoken bond of trust that whatever he let happen to me would bring me only pleasure. Nervous anticipation, of course, and sometimes a little enjoyable panic, but never fright. Yet despite myself, I knew in my heart that the leaping levels of fear Jeanne's behaviour kept bringing me to were also exciting far beyond anything I had ever experienced. The sight of her red hair brushing against my stomach as she bent over me to help the man, just to speed up the removal of my corset, her pink-tipped breasts just touching my own, filled me with burgeoning pleasure.

And then a minute later she was upright, the brush in her hand, and she advanced and smiled ever so nicely at me as she brought the back of the brush down hard on the outside of my right thigh. It burned and stung – how it stung! – and as the next 'thwack' landed seconds later, tears rolled from the corners of my eyes into my ears, but I was determined that this time I would not make a sound. Jeanne looked almost disappointed, but I decided to be grateful she had spared me the bristles. She brought the brush down harder and harder and I sucked air in sharply despite myself, but I didn't cry out. Jeanne held the brush in the air for a horrible, long moment and then brought it down on the inside of my wide-spread thigh this time. Anticipating each fresh slap of the wooden brush, my thighs were rigid with tension, but I made no sound, even though the pain increased with every stroke on my poor tender skin. Jeanne's eyes searched mine and I held her gaze, tears still running down my face into my hair and onto the pillow, my face as flushed pink as I was sure the skin on my legs must be, and I willed her silently not to hurt my breasts in spite.

I began to think I couldn't bear it much longer, that the soft skin of my inner thigh could not take such a beating for another minute, when she stopped abruptly and ran a hand across my stomach. Holding my breath, I watched as Jeanne moved back again and bent down between my legs. I clenched my thighs involuntarily again, before I felt an unnerving, gentle warmth on my abandoned pussy. It took a moment to realise that this was the warmth of Jeanne's mouth, and I was full of gratitude, but before I could relax into the feeling she stopped and motioned to the man.

'Do you know,' she said chattily to him, 'I think she's getting the hang of it?'

'Are you sure?' he asked. 'I don't want to take any risks.'

'Let's test her,' suggested Jeanne, and climbed swiftly and gracefully across my body to untie the bindings, first at each wrist, and then at each ankle. I so badly wanted to curl up into a ball to protect myself, to rub and soothe each point where I had been tied and on the sore, spanked places, but more than that I did not want to start the whole painful process again.

'Try her now,' offered Jeanne, passing him the hair-brush. I lay motionless, and offered no resistance as the man moved round the bed to face me, grasped my splayed legs and tugged me further down towards my erotic tormentors.

I felt again her quick little hands hold me open, and an object pushing at the opening of my pussy. Warmer and thicker than I was expecting, I looked straight into the man's face and as he grimaced with pleasure, breathing out a loud sigh of relief, I realised that he was still holding the hairbrush and that finally I was being filled and fucked by a real person. His hands instinctively reached for my hips and he pulled me roughly closer to him as he began to thrust more quickly into me. I was so desperate for the pleasure of orgasm to distract me from the pain in other parts of my body that I hardly minded the way he touched me, ignoring me mostly as though I were nothing but an object. I looked for Jeanne who stood beside him and noticed her odd expression. Her face was flushed in a way it had not been five minutes earlier, and her breathing was harder.

'Get off her,' she murmured. When he ignored her, she leant across and hissed in his ear, 'Get the fuck off her!'

He froze immediately, but his cock remained hard as rock buried deep inside me. 'Get out,' said Jeanne again, quietly and more menacingly than before. To my disappointment, he pulled out of me, leaving my legs dangling over the edge of the bed and my pussy feeling empty. I almost cried out with the unfairness of Jeanne's behaviour, but with a huge effort I restrained myself, pressing my mouth and eyes closed shut.

And then Jeanne was upon me. The first thing I felt was her mouth on mine, pushing my lips open and licking my tongue with hers, passion and heat suddenly replacing her glacial cruelty. Without thinking, I reached up and took her narrow frame in my arms, stroking her satin hair and velvet skin, and she let me roll her over and run my hands crazily over her skin, her breasts, stomach, legs. I wanted to please her, to slow down and caress her properly, but I was filled with a sense of sudden abandon, desperate to take her in, taste and enjoy her body all at once. Frenziedly I reached for her breasts again, bending my head to suck her nipples in turn, biting them gently and then more roughly, her fingertips up and down my own back, pulling me close and encouraging me. Instinctively I reached down to slide my hand between her slim thighs, fingers slipping effortlessly deep into the hot wetness of her pussy. I drew back onto all fours to see her properly and to spread her thighs to see more clearly what she had seen of me before, and heard the man groan despite himself, a dreadful noise full of pain and frustration, and I turned for just a second to encourage him too. Even after all that had happened I decided I could not let him suffer as he had let me suffer, and as I plunged my soaking fingers to and fro inside Jeanne's gorgeously plump and tight pussy, I felt him grasp my bottom as firmly as my hips before, steady himself for barely a moment and then thrust himself hard to the hilt in my own aching, slippery, grateful cunt. Jeanne bucked and thrust herself at my eager palm, and I turned my hand to slide my thumb against her clit as my fingers twisted and pulled inside her, making her cry out, her beautiful green eyes staring into mine as the man shoved and fucked and thrust at me, grasping my swinging breasts to steady himself and pinching a nipple hard in the process until I could hardly control myself. Jeanne's pale skin shone in the candlelight and her cries grew louder until, blissfully, I felt her begin to shudder, her whole body racked with a pleasure that made me give in too, melting and juddering and trying to hold myself together enough to sustain her as I felt the man's final, faster thrusts as he groaned and crushed out of me his last throbs of ecstasy and we fell together, a heap of sweat and disarray and guilty, satisfied grins.

You liked that, didn't you? – No, don't move. Don't you dare move. I can see you're very excited. You can't move an inch, not until I tell you to. You'll just have to wait until I say you can touch yourself again. Until I untie you. And the more you complain, the longer you'll have to wait until I do.

GRAMMAR LESSON

I arrive punctually. The chateau is whitewashed with wet slate roof tiles that shine in the sudden autumn sun. Virginia creeper slings it's scarlet arms around the door. I am nervous as I climb the steps. This is my first time.

You have brown eyes, round as a puppy's, and short rough hair. Your smile opens like a gate. I hear the latch click. I want to come in. You are. You are much younger than I am and eager to learn.

He is a student.

She is a teacher.

The past simple is used for completed action. I moved to France. I got a job teaching English. I was not happy. You slouched opposite my desk and I told you to sit up straight and concentrate. You did, which surprised me.

Grammar Lesson

I recommended you for extra lessons.

The past continuous is used for interrupted action. I was waiting for something to happen. You were being good. *It is also used for action that happens around a certain time.* I was thinking about you this morning. You were thinking about me just then.

You were having a shower. I let myself in with the key you gave me and stood at your bedroom door. I could smell your peppermint soap and see wreaths of steam about the ceiling. The clothes you dropped in a heap on the floor still carried a faint trace of heat from your body. The cotton was soft and worn.

I sat on the bed. You knew I was there. You walked into the room naked.

Your teeth are white as milk and a dark ridge of hair runs straight down your belly from your navel. *The present simple is used to express general truth.* You are beautiful. You are seventeen. You are confident and powerful and utterly yourself. I want you to fuck me.

You say nothing as you kneel on the rug in front of me. I dig my fingers into the back of your dripping crew cut and bring your mouth to mine. Your tongue tries unfamiliar shapes. Your lips test fricatives. You press your damp body against my charcoal suit. I do not want to get undressed. You slip your thumbs into the waistband and pull up my skirt, frowning in concentration. You remove my jacket and undo my silk shirt like you're gutting something, with sharp brutal movements. I chose to relinquish underwear.

I am rain that falls with increasing force. You are stone, unlined by time.

The present continuous can be used for action that is not yet complete. I am winding my legs around your waist. You are holding my wrists and forcing me backwards, testing your strength. I am feeling a desperate weight of wanting you, but I have no idea what you are feeling as you slam your loins into mine.

I am going to come. You are going to come. *This is called the 'going to' future.* Your eyelashes flutter against my cheek. Too soon. The clasp of my bracelet scratches your neck. I push you away and you look – for a moment – abashed, beaten, confused.

The single duvet slides from the bed as I roll you on your back on the polished floor. The tops of the fir trees nod inquisitively from the edge of your parents' garden. A deep-voiced guard dog barks a warning. I touch you everywhere except where you want to be touched. I take the thick third finger of your left hand in my mouth. I stroke the hollows of your armpits and trace the curves of the muscles of your arms. I lay my head on your heart. You wait to exhale. I run the tip of my tongue down the plane of your stomach. The ends of my hair flick your groin and you twitch, emitting a low growl.

Grammar Lesson

I have seen you race bare-fleet-footed on the packed earth. I blow gently along the inside of your thigh, making you squirm. *The present perfect is used for action that has just concluded.* You have had enough. *It is also used for action continuing to the present.* I have noticed your determination. You are not used to deferment. I am older but you are stronger. You leap up and push me against the wall in one graceful movement. A drawing pin drops to the ground.

Your broad upper body rams me. Your breath rips close to my ear. My skirt, riding about my hips, is torn in our scrum. You wrap your fist in my tumbled locks and nail me to the spot. When you bite my shoulder it feels like you are gnawing bone. You make me gasp. You make me shudder. You make me come. I am aware of your face, shadow of beard and smudge of freckles across the bridge of the nose, inches from mine. You are watching intently, gauging my reaction to your movements, studying how best to please the teacher.

I do not know how to sprint, ski, skateboard or speak French and I have forgotten everything I ever used to think I knew. This is new. I fold around you. My hungry lips mumble your tongue; my warm cunt welcomes you like coming home. You take my right hand and cover it palm to palm with your left, securing it against the wall. You do the same with my left and I realise how much taller you are than I am, even in my heels. Our heads droop sweet as turtledoves, eyes closed, scenting, nose to tender crook of sweat-pearled neck, taking breath. And so we hang, mutually crucified…

When you release your grip and dip to kiss between my legs, my arms remain raised, wrists twined together, knotted in an agony of wanting and forgetting. You are on your knees again. I lean against the wall with the posters of Led Zeppelin on it. Your fingertips dig into the tops of my thighs where eight bruises will bloom and I will remember their planting as something precious. You bite. I sigh. You grind your teeth against my jutting hipbone and span the width of my hips with your hands. Moving lower, you hook a thumb in my dark wet cleft and suckle my clit. The scent of wet turf rises. Outside the lawns spread emerald green.

With the future tense two auxiliaries are used, depending on a sense of command or promise on the part of the verb subject (although there are exceptions). I will go denotes intention. I shall go is mere futurity.

I wonder what you will remember of this lesson, this day, of me… *'Will,' of course, is also used for prediction.* You will be a great man. You will recall nothing of these events but the envelope left on the hall table, which I shall pocket as my fee.

OUR MUTUAL SATISFACTION

I hadn't given you a second look when our eyes first made contact in that City pub. And when I say it was a pub, I mean it was a centuries-old shady cavern soaked in memories of a London past – not one of those blonde wood and chromium franchised dining rooms that, in recent years, have sprouted up near office complexes calling themselves bars. The majority of my colleagues, being designers in their late twenties and early thirties, habitually gravitate towards Shoreditch, famous for its coterie of trendy drinking holes but, on a crisp midwinter evening, when it's dark by 4.30 p.m., it's just so comforting to be settling in the penumbra of an ancient pub. I don't want to stand exposed on polished, laminate floors in spot-lit, smoke-free environments; I prefer the intimate feel of the booth, the barrel for a table in the cosy dark corner, the low ceiling built in the eighteenth century, and an environment designed for storytelling and gentle inebriation. Claustrophobic for some, but much more conducive to seduction, I'm sure you'll agree.

I hadn't given you a second look because you were walking past me carrying a pint of beer in each hand. I was doing the same, headed towards the corner of the pub where a few of us were already a couple of drinks into Friday evening revelry, thoughts of the weekend lifting our mood. By the time I had delivered the drinks, you were somewhere over the other side of the room, and it wasn't going to be possible to make eye contact again unless one of us was particularly bold. There was nothing unusual in my being looked at; men look at me – at all women – all the time, biology alerting their eyes to make lightning-quick tallies of fuckability: age; hip to waist ratio, gloss of hair and shine of eye. But it is rare that the gaze penetrates so deep into one's psyche, especially from a glance lasting a fraction of a heartbeat.

The workplace banter was cheery and it was good to be one of the gang, but I knew as I sat down among my colleagues that a lustful interest in a stranger had been sparked and, from thereon in, attention to my colleagues' anecdotes was not 100 per cent. I started drifting on girly reveries about us being a couple. And thinking what you might be like under that Gieves and Hawkes single-breasted pin stripe. From that brief glance I had noticed you were slim, in shape, had healthy skin. The likelihood of us having anything in common was remote, though. You were a suit and I was a party-loving designer in an ad agency. We would never be able to stomach each other's iPod playlist, and you would no doubt be appalled by my behaviour at festivals, getting battered and dancing like a maniac. But the whole thing was ridiculous anyway, going off on flights of fancy when all that had happened was that I'd been on the receiving end of a casual glance. A glance loaded with erotic suggestion – at least that's how I'd interpreted it.

I amused myself with the capricious notion of acting outrageously in front of you – playing the tease to your buttoned-down conservative. What fun that would be, dancing just out of your reach; driving you wild with a little routine, dressed in my cute gingham and lace push-up bra and flouncy pants that I happened to be wearing that day, my firm flesh filling the wholesome material just fine. All this tumbled into my head in the flash of a moment. What had you done? You had managed to turn me on in a pub with one second's look into my eyes. I was the most aroused I'd been in months. It was crazy.

My colleagues were laughing, each telling tales of adventure, the topic for some reason being 'the worst guesthouse I've ever stayed in.' Characterful stories were flying around, of nightmare b&bs and the shocker of other guests' bedroom antics filtering through wafer-thin walls. I was already on my way to being half-woozy, so I launched into telling the story of the Welsh farmhouse I'd stayed in, where the husband and wife proprietors had taken an unhealthy interest in my marital status, making inappropriate jokes about rural boredom and how nice it would be if they knew more 'fun-loving young people'. Then the conversation turned to statistics about swinging and dogging and any number of adult practices that are supposed to be going on in suburban homes. I couldn't bring myself to join in the cynical snipes; I was all too aware of how aroused I had become, heady and flushed from the full-bodied red wine and in a carefree mood, enough to initiate a little flirting.

I had finished my drink, so I assumed you would be doing the same. I was seized then with the panic that you might be leaving very soon, keen to get your train home to wifey. Of course you would be married. You looked in your mid-forties. Few men as well turned out as you are single at that age unless they are gay. My ego needed more of your admiring gaze; I was in exhibitionist mode. I wanted to feel your eyes roaming over my body. I would entice you with my shiny hair, my lips, my breasts. I would at least place myself in close proximity to you before my next drink was in front of me.

I went to the loos to freshen my make-up – to slick on some sparkling lip gloss; to dust highlighter over my cheeks; to sleek my hair into a shining curtain. I knew I was looking good, delighted with myself for choosing that day to wear one of my most cleavage-enhancing tops. I was feeling that giddy brazenness that comes after a few drinks and the knowledge you can lie-in the next morning. But what would I do exactly? Stand beside your table like an idiot? Hang around at the bar hoping to catch your eye? Too random. I came out of the ladies and the solution was staring me in the face. The menu board. Oh joy! It was placed at right angles to the bar, and I correctly guessed that was where you were seated.

Affecting innocence, I walked into your lair to stand before the chalkboard. I had about one minute to draw you to me, and I'd better make it good. Disaster would have been coming away from there with a bowl of chips and a steak sandwich. Triumph would have to ensue, precipitated by the angle of my hip to waist ratio and the slight tilt of my body as I rested one knee on a vacant stool, side on to your field of vision. You were with two sober men of equally smart dress and demeanour. Whatever you were discussing, it certainly wasn't the frivolous speculation of what a Welsh farmer might have done on finding your pants tangled into his bedsheets. My smart skirt rose above my knee to reveal dark woollen stockings that stopped just short of the thigh, with a soft and silky inch of girl flesh put temptingly on display. And still I concentrated on the menu, before angling my head to one side and then catching you exactly where I wanted you – looking at me.

I smiled shyly and cheered inside with the realisation that you had been trapped by the bait. All I had to do was wait for the approach. Out of the corner of my eye I saw you mutter something to the other men. They had finished their drinks and were collecting themselves to leave. No, no, not you, I pleaded to myself. And, sure as you like, my plea was answered. Free of your corporate companions, you sidled up to me. It was at that instant, without a word having been exchanged, that I knew how things would progress. I instinctively understood I could inflame you to a senseless passion by paying you scant regard. You didn't want a garrulous floozy fawning over you. So I kept my attention fixed on the board. No one could *prove* I was soliciting your company as shamelessly as a hooker; or that I was nothing other than a horny slut hungry for cock. Of course not. I was a young professional suddenly taken peckish, checking out the food on offer in this well-frequented public house, with its legendary steak sandwiches. I knew you knew the bluff, and the game was on.

I could feel the heat radiating from your suit as you approached me with a confidence that spoke of your mastery of situations loaded with promise. Your opening gambit was to announce something flippant about one of the dishes, but I still resisted looking at you. There was something provocative and perverse about denying myself the face to face contact I had craved, but I dragged it out to the point where it would have been insolent to do otherwise. As the heat intensified and the air around us was almost buzzing, I slowly turned towards you, making sure to lift my skirt with both hands for just a second before I slid my leg off the stool and righted myself on two feet.

I stood close in front of you, and there it was again! I felt the punch of arousal in my solar plexus as powerful as if you had done nothing less than drive into me there and then. So private a moment, but so deliciously forbidden to be experiencing it with a stranger. And in a public place. And so early in the proceedings.

'And are you actually going to order anything?' you asked, a wry smirk on your face betraying your awareness of my intention to order absolutely nothing besides perhaps another drink.

'What do you recommend?' I continued the futile dialogue around food. I had plenty of conversation on the topic in reserve, in case I had completely misjudged the situation and you were merely being friendly.

'That you temper your hunger for just a while longer. That we nip across the road to the Great Eastern Hotel and justify what's occurring here.'

Oh joy. You had been happy to suggest it. To make the moves. A gentleman by appearance and action. You didn't leave the ignominy to me. I didn't have to expose myself as the harlot I so obviously was. I could relax enough to jest at the spontaneity.

'As long as we can eat *fairly* soon,' I ventured, looking up with a devilish expression into your handsome face. 'It's winter, and I need to keep the engine stoked.'

You smiled at the emphasis I placed on that last word.

'So you agree… we'll leave now.' You said it as a decision and not a question.

I moved rapidly to my colleagues' table and grabbed my coat, muttering breathlessly that I had to go. I'd just run into someone I knew and we simply had to have a heart to heart. Blah blah. No one cared. Instead I got the 'have a lovely weekend' farewells and that was it. I was off into the night without a second thought to what I was about to do. But my intuition told me it was the right thing.

The couple of blocks we had to walk passed by in a haze of anticipation, where time doesn't so much as stand still as whizz along at a furious rate. It was one of those wild nights of abandon and glee, where London feels like the most dynamic place on earth; when the air is intoxicating and a young woman is radiant from knowing she is desired. You took my hand, your stride longer than mine, so I could indulge myself with the feeling that I was being dragged to your bed in that smart hotel.

You were a man of the world that night – making your claim on a coveted thing soon to be in your possession. Your every move was direct and determined. You were someone who would neither fuss nor fumble. I was giddy with the waiting for your hands upon me, knowing that I would stretch out the play until the final moment. It would drive us both to the edge of reason, and all the while I would feed upon your desire for me. It would replenish me for weeks to come.

A rush of warmth enveloped me as you led me into the swanky reception area of your hotel. It was perfect. All golden glow and deep-pile carpet and anonymity assured. The lift arrived with a comforting 'ping' and we ascended to your floor. I took the opportunity of the dead time in the lift to be skittish, running my hands over my body, when we both knew I'd rather it were yours doing the same. Again, the torture of denial and procrastination was like a fever. We would soon fall upon each other like supernatural beings, dependent on the life force of erotic energy. We were both desperate for the exquisite conclusion, but we knew, unspoken, that we would savour every second of its postponement.

Into the room and the view was magical – a twinkling London skylight with all the landmark buildings visible. Your suite was positively palatial. It struck me as comic irony that earlier I had been discussing the worst rural guesthouses and here I was in a luxury room in the heart of the city. I fought hard with myself to stop blurting out the usual excuses – 'I've never done this before' – 'I hope you won't think I'm too much of a slut,' etc. Instead, I bravely continued the sport, turning the questions on you, asking you if you did this regularly, if you often go home with the first woman that makes overtures in an evening.

At your age, perhaps fifteen years older than me, it would be naïve to think that you hadn't acted on impulse on numerous occasions, but you were enough of a gentleman to tell me the feeling had never before been so instant, so strong. You were saying all the right things. And talking to me from across the room. I was standing, leaning on the dressing table; I didn't want to sit down. To my mind, seduction is best instigated vertically. It allows more possibilities for grand gestures, making the best of one's body language. To arch my back and maximise the curvature of my female form while seated is pointless if no one can see the effect it has on my bottom.

You were drawn to me, had taken off the suit jacket but made no attempt to loosen your tie. In one sudden, determined movement, your hands rushed up my smart skirt and felt their way hungrily around my thighs and the undercurve of my buttocks. Your fingers grazed the flounce of my gingham panties, feeling the snug cut of their fit on my flesh, and you leant further against me. I braced myself, my arms stretched out behind me as I revelled in your exploration. It was a form of worship. Your reaction was blissfully promising, pressing an urgency into my pelvis.

'We're not going to have these off just yet,' you said, flicking the elastic of my panties against my hip.

'And what about this?' I flicked at your tie and your suit trousers and shirt.

'The man's prerogative to keep on, if he so desires,' was the answer.

It transpired you wanted a striptease. Despite your arousal you were controlled and mature enough to make everything perfect; not rushing into the proceedings like an adolescent. The mini-bar was opened.

You poured vodka tonics, dimmed the lights and settled back into the velvet chair to watch the show. Without any discussion, you had tapped in to my fantasy – of showing off unashamedly, being a private dancer for an audience of one gorgeous professional man. Both of us, straight from our offices, were dressed for the boardroom rather than the back streets, and the delicious incongruity of ribald behaviour and lustful intent under tailored clothes was brought to its apogee.

You found a radio station with instrumental music – lyrics are so intrusive in such circumstances – and I found myself eager to perform. I moved around the room, making the most of the furniture, rolling on the bed and writhing on the floor towards you as you sat, fully erect, sipping your drink and occasionally asking for particular fancies. I was shameless with the heady indulgence of it all. By the time I got down to bra and knickers you could stand no more and pulled me to sit on your lap where you caressed me, bending me forwards on all fours once or twice to run your hands over the firm fleshy contents of those cute gingham panties.

When you released yourself I was stopped short in my tracks to fall upon you and work you with moist dexterity. I devoured and honoured you, my own form of worship. All the coquettish play and the conversational subtext were to be justified in the very serious business of release. I sat back and admired you in your state of undoing. By this time the tie had been loosened, the shoes were off and you were about to surrender to the deep hot sweetness.

Before I could think what to do next, you seized me and dragged me to the bed by my wrists. Again I allowed myself the naughty thought that I was being taught a lesson – so wanton was my behaviour, with all that squirming around in a gentleman's bedroom, that it was not to be tolerated a moment longer. I was thrown onto the bed with such force that I bounced, giggling and feeling as ripe and female as I had ever felt. All the dressing up and the flirting and pouting and dancing was all worth it for this rush.

You slid one arm around my waist and pulled me to the side of the bed. This was not to be a skin on skin experience which, curiously, added to the thrill. The emotional intimacy that comes out of nakedness would not have been right for this, for now. You whipped down the panties and held me there against you at the edge of the bed as your fingers helped themselves to the juicy cloying furnace the core of me had become. I then turned into an adult starlet, risking a few spoken obscenities which enflamed you further to work harder, as I wound my toned bare legs around you. It felt so deliciously thrilling to be almost naked against your dressed form.

As I came to my ecstasy I knew I would have to look into your eyes, to get the punch that would spill me into voluptuous oblivion. It was the same look I'd seen on first sight, but for much longer and more intently as, in the dying moments of my orgasm, you allowed yourself the prize. The suit trousers were released and you were fully available.

With vigour and a sense of needing to claim your part of the experience, you then drove into me with a passion I'd not experienced in my thirty years. The contrast to your daily persona was dizzying – as if you were tapping into the sexual energies to bring about an almost supernatural transformation. Suit to brute in sixty seconds, to relish as essential that which is too often rendered mundane. It was a shameless enjoyment of the animal moment and you were as much of a beast as I'd hoped.

Your touch was so firm, so perfect, so primal. Not knowing you actually made it easier for me to let go. I didn't have to worry that I would even see you again. I could be as uncensored as I wanted. Your stranger status, the anonymity of the hotel suite, all conspired to make sensational the moment that had been brewing in my body.

It was to our mutual satisfaction, after all.

THE LECTURE

Clare chewed at the corner of her pink, polished fingernail as she scanned the hotel lobby. A waitress came by offering another drink which she declined with a distracted half-smile on her lips. She huffed and fell back into the velvet banquette, wishing she had brought a newspaper. Glancing at her wrist watch, she noted that she'd been waiting thirty-five minutes already. Now she remembered Naomi's habitual lateness. The urge to flee mounted in her chest. At what point was it reasonable to leave?

'My God, you look delicious,' a throaty voice exclaimed. 'Mmm. Just like a ripe apricot.'

Clare flushed to the roots of her rose-gold hair. 'Naomi...'

Naomi dropped an enormous shopping bag and

slipped in beside Clare. She curled her legs beneath and settled into a sleek, feline pose. She leaned back and took in her old friend with huge ebony eyes. Reaching out to stroke Clare's freckled cheek with a slim, tapered finger she murmured, 'I'm so happy to see you, it's been too long.'

Clare basked in the glow of Naomi's attention. The tight spring of anxious irritation she had experienced moments before uncoiled as they slipped quickly into a bubble of loquacious intimacy. At the end of university, their relationship had been strained when Naomi mistook her admiring crush for something deeper, but this reunion felt fine, the closeness without the complications. As they chatted, Clare was suddenly shocked to feel Naomi's hand reaching into her skirt and up between her thighs. It paused and firmly grasped the warm, giving flesh at the top of Clare's stockings. Gasping, she recalled, as well, the electric current that had always run between them.

Naomi's eyelids were dark and hooded. She wanted Clare with a vengeance. She snaked her fingers under Clare's panties and into the folds of her pussy. Clare's nostrils flared like a pony's. She involuntarily pushed her mound into Naomi's palm. A hard smile flickered across Naomi's deeply rouged lips.

Naomi closed in on Clare, nipped her earlobe between her teeth, and revved up the speed of her deft hand in Clare's slickening crotch. 'You're a dirty little girl, aren't you?' she whispered as Clare whimpered and threw back her head, her pleasure mounting.

'Can I get you anything?' a waitress surprised them, breaking the spell. Clare stammered, red-faced, while Naomi looked up and casually ordered another round of cocktails, still circling Clare's clitoris under the table.

Clare squeezed her thighs together and squirmed to adjust her skirt under the table. 'We can't do this.' Naomi grinned, satisfied, for now, simply by Clare's state of arousal. 'Whatever you say.' She flicked her fingertip with her tongue. 'So sweet…'

The waitress returned with their drinks. 'Don't let me have too many of these. I have to be up in front of five hundred ridiculously eager students in a stuffy auditorium at 10 a.m. tomorrow morning.'

'Ah, yes,' said Claire, desperately trying to ignore the emphatic pulse between her legs. She inhaled slowly. 'Tell me all about the lecture.'

Naomi pulled a flyer out of her vintage black patent-leather clutch and tossed it on the table. Clare squinted slightly and then put on a pair of cats-eye reading glasses.

'Those suit you,' purred Naomi. 'Very "sexy librarian".'

The card featured a photograph of Naomi with her

hair pulled back sharply off her angular cheekbones. She was wearing a dark tailored suit with a severely nipped-in waist and a tight pencil skirt.

'The crusty old boys in the Ivory Tower seem to find it a turn-on when I get suited up like a warden in the all-girl prison of their dreams. But tomorrow, I think I'll surprise them.' She riffled through the tissue paper in her shopping bag and withdrew a long swathe of bias-cut plum charmeuse. Clare imagined the dress slinking over Naomi's sinuous body. 'Still, if this doesn't say "Pussy Power" I don't know what does.'

Clare read aloud: '*De-constructing Sexual Hegemonies*. My goodness, I've been out of school so long, I can't even imagine what that means.'

'I could give you a private tutorial,' Naomi shot back.

Clare blanched, 'Please, Naomi...'

She patted Clare's hand reassuringly. 'Oh, I'm just kidding. Its actually a bunch of academic bullshit. Ugh. I'd rather be doing Emma Bovary or something,' she added disparagingly, and then chuckled to herself, 'and I mean that literally... but, really, this is what keeps me in my Louboutins.' She stretched out a willowy leg and rotated her foot for inspection. She was wearing towering black stilettos with studded straps that snaked up her ankle gladiator-style.

Clare hesitantly reached out toward Naomi's knee.

'You do look amazing…'

Naomi crossed her leg, angling it away from Clare, 'Yes, well, you do too. Must be that man of yours,' she said crisply, 'tell me all about him.'

'But, what about you, are you in a relationship?' Clare asked, with a falsely bright note in her voice. She leaned forward intently.

Naomi wrinkled her nose. 'Oh, these lesbians today. All they want to do is get married and have babies. Appalling.'

It was now the dinner hour and the hotel lobby had emptied of tourists and of business people meeting for after-work drinks. The lights were lowered and a waitress placed a votive candle on their table. She handed them each a menu of *meze* dishes. 'Why not? I'm ravenous.' Naomi said. 'But what about whashis-name… Jack? Were you planning to eat with him?'

'He probably has to work late. He's installing a new show at the gallery.'

'Call him. Make him come. It will be fun, I promise. I won't bite.'

Clare smiled. 'OK, why not?' She pulled out her mobile phone. 'I'll call from outside.'

When Clare returned, Naomi had already ordered something to eat for them.

'He can't make it for a little while, but he said he'd join us for dessert.' In a moment, the waitress returned carrying a big Moroccan silver tray piled with delectable bits of food. Naomi placed an olive between her lips and sucked and nibbled at it with her small, sharp, white teeth until the pit was perfectly clean.

'Now, before he arrives, we have to cover all the important stuff… like, how is he in the sack?'

Clare attempted to look scandalized, but then after she considered the question for a moment, her face softened. She weighed a soft, heavy fig in her fingertips. 'Honestly… he's gorgeous and passionate and loves sex, but he hasn't given me an orgasm.' She bit hard into the fruit and held Naomi's gaze.

Naomi snorted, 'That won't do! I'd give him a couple of weeks to meet his potential or else he's fired.' The women laughed conspiratorily. Clare felt easy again, pleasantly full and tipsy. At that moment, a tall blond man in a well-cut jacket strode toward them across the room. 'You must be the famous roommate!'

'Speak of the Devil,' Naomi replied, grabbing his hand and pulling him down to sit across from her. 'You just missed all the wonderful things your lover was saying about you.'

Clare was suddenly nervous. Jack looked so stiff. His face was highly coloured and eyes burning like lanterns. He did feel a bit panicked meeting this person he had heard so much about, the woman who had captivated Clare when she was younger. He had not quite realized, as he now observed, that their bond was this intense. But little by little, he relaxed, entertained by her jokes and gossip.

As Naomi shared a salty rumour about a certain sought-after young artist's outlandish proclivities in bed, her leg brushed his. Her unshod foot began running up and down the inside of his calf. He glanced at Clare, she looked oblivious, just pleased to have the two of them getting along. He threw back his single malt as Naomi's foot wormed its way up his thigh and pushed between his legs. The arch fit perfectly over the curved form of his hardening penis.

Clare was beginning to feel left out of their art world banter. She motioned to Jack that it was getting late.

'But we promised him dessert!' Naomi protested, rubbing Jack's cock insistently. 'If you're tired, let's go to my room and order something from room service – I'll call you a cab from there.'

'Come on darling, you haven't seen your friend in years,' Jack cajoled. Clare acquiesced. A bit piqued, she decided she wasn't going to let the night end with Jack getting all the attention.

The room was decorated entirely in shades of pinky beige. A channel-stitched satin quilt covered the bed. Heavy pleated curtains had been drawn across the windows, giving the small chamber the feel of a capsule detached from time and space.

'It's so cosy,' Clare said, angling to reconnect with her friend. 'Very double x chromosome.'

'Yes, a veritable "Womb of One's Own",' Naomi joked, as she tossed her shoes onto the thick, velvety rug. She bent down to ransack the mini-bar. She grabbed a half bottle of Moët, tiny bottles of cognac, and a box of Belgian chocolates. 'Help yourselves. It's all covered by the lecture expenses.' She eased down onto the bed with the goodies.

Clare stretched out beside her, tasting a chocolate. She held it out to Jack. 'Here, you finish this, you like sticky, sweet stuff.'

Naomi patted the bed. 'Come on, join us.' The cocktails were now catching up with Clare and she smiled hazily at Jack and made space for him on the bed. She no longer felt irked, instead she had the impulse to baby him. 'He's such a hard worker, I think he deserves to be spoiled. You look like you need a massage. Doesn't he Naomi?'

Naomi knelt beside him. 'Absolutely. Now, off with the shirt, time for a back rub.'

Jack smiled wickedly, unbuttoning his starched oxford. 'I won't argue with that.' He lay on his stomach. Naomi instructed Clare to sit astride his waist. She hiked up her skirt and climbed over his back. His skin felt pleasantly hot and smooth beneath her thighs. She worked on the muscles that ridged his spine and noted with a slightly dizzy feeling, that Naomi was simultaneously kneading his shoulders. Naomi reached for the champagne. She popped the cork and let a tiny rivulet trickle down the deep cleft between his vertebrae. Clare leaned over and licked at the yeasty bubbles, her hair brushing against his skin. Jack moaned softly.

Naomi crawled on hands and knees around behind Clare and said in a mock whisper, 'I think we need to get rid of the pants, too.' She ran her hand over the contours of his firm buttocks and in between his thighs, causing him to lift his hips in response. With her other hand, she quickly reached beneath him, unbuttoning his trousers and swiftly pulling them off.

Jack turned over so Clare was seated on his firm belly. 'Not fair. What about you two?' He slid his hands onto the lobes of her buttocks and rocked her pubic bone into him. She could feel his cock pushing into the small of her back. She returned the pressure languorously.

Naomi untied the belt of the silky wrap dress she was wearing, let it fall to the floor, and sat back on the bed. 'You'll see, I always play fair.' Clare could make out her maroon nipples jutting against the black cups of her demi-bra.

Clare's heart banged against her ribcage. She rolled

off Jack and lay on her back between them. He leaned over and kissed her neck and collarbone while undoing the buttons on her blouse.

Slowly, Naomi pulled down Clare's skirt. 'She's gorgeous, isn't she? Look at this tummy.' She caressed Clare's sloped, ivory belly. Jack nuzzled her breasts and sucked at a rosy nipple. Naomi lay on her side and stretched her body against Clare. She began stroking Clare's neck with her tongue. Clare arched her head back, exposing her throat. She felt like she was spinning, and closed her eyes. She let her mind go empty. Her hips began to rise and fall with their own rhythm and Naomi reached into her knickers and pushed the heel of her hand into the curls of her pussy and slipped her fingers between her wet lips. Clare turned over to face Naomi and the women's legs entwined. Jack rubbed his cock over the fine mesh covering Clare's buttocks and kissed and bit the back of her neck hungrily. Clare felt Naomi's mouth on hers. It was full and giving and tasted lightly of salt. She pressed her sex hard into Naomi's thigh and wrapped her arms around the other woman's back, pulling her closer. Naomi arched toward her, catching Clare's hand and pushing it between her legs. Clare let out a sob of pleasure.

Jack had let himself flow with the girls' attention and was thrilled to see Clare loosen up, but the sound of Naomi pleasuring her now overwhelmed him. He felt left out and couldn't handle it. He flew off the bed and bolted into the bathroom without looking back. The women untangled themselves and sat up. Clare grasped at the bedspread and pulled it over herself. 'What have I done?' she whined, thinking about how stupidly jealous Jack could be.

'Don't worry.' Naomi said. 'I'll take care of it.' And before Clare could respond, she stood up and glided toward the bathroom. Clare was paralyzed for a moment, but couldn't bear lying there helpless and left out. What could Naomi be saying to him? She padded toward the door. She heard Naomi's voice.

'That's right. Open it as gently as you would the wings of a butterfly. Now just blow softly. Tease it awake.'

Clare peeked into the room. There was Naomi, her pretty bottom perched on the white marble counter and her head leaning back against the mirror. Jack was kneeling on the floor in front of her and her knees were thrown wide and ankles resting on his muscular shoulders. Naomi murmured, 'I'm going to give you a lesson now. Listen carefully. Lightly lick the inner lips. Yes, like that – flick along the edges. Now, more. Lap deep into the crevices.' Clare stood stunned watching him so compliant, on his knees before this woman.

'Do you feel how hot you're making me? Run your

tongue up, up again and onto my clitoris. Open me. Just like that. Softly move your tongue over the little pearl. That's right... you're making me want something inside. Put your finger in me. Mmm... stroke me with that long finger. Do you feel that soft spot deep inside? Rub it. Keep licking. ... Yes... like that.' Her voice was becoming ragged.

Clare watched icily as Naomi began to grind her hips uncontrollably. His hand was moving in and out of her faster and faster. She could see his hard cock hovering and twitching. But gradually, as she heard Naomi's raw little cries, she began to melt. Her toes. Up her calves and thighs. Her insides felt hot and liquid. She realised he was making her friend come, for her.

Naomi let out moan after moan and squeezed her eyes shut, grimacing. Eventually, her legs relaxed. She caught her breath. 'Now show her what I taught you,' she instructed.

Jack stood up and, turning to see his girlfriend, led Clare to the bed. He laid her down so that her hips were just on the edge. He kissed and fondled her on the outside of her underwear making her crave more contact. The skin on her thighs began to quiver. It seemed to her that she might drown. She tried to snap her knees closed, but persistently he forced them apart. He grabbed the crotch of her knickers and tore them open and probed her teasingly with his tongue. She pushed his head away with her hands, but he grabbed her wrists and held them down. The struggle excited her; nothing was in her control anymore. Her whole body tensed and then started to vibrate out from her core.

'She wants you.' Naomi breathed. He climbed on top of Clare, pushing his cock decisively inside her. Her muscles rippled around him. She threw her arms around his neck and drew him in farther. They moved together, each stroke bringing her higher.

Naomi came up behind him. She had strapped a leather harness over her crotch which was lashed tightly around her with thin cords of leather. To this she attached a slim dildo made of clear black resin. First he could feel her stroking and opening his cheeks gently with her fingers. With one hand she cradled and caressed his balls and with the other she guided the shaft slowly up into him. He winced for a moment and then let himself submit to the erotic shock of being taken.

Naomi rode him like a horse, all the while exhorting his movement inside the other woman. Clare rapturously felt them butting against her in tandem, forcing her to the edge of a precipice. She cried out and let herself leap. Wave after wave of impossible pleasure surged over her body. Jack felt as if Clare's pussy were gripping him and turning him inside out. He kneaded her breasts and groaned into her neck. His entire skin was prickly and on fire. As Naomi continued to work at his ass and his balls, he came in a frenzy of sensation that rolled through the deepest parts of his body and coursed out of him like a red-hot shot.

The three collapsed and lay limp like discarded marionettes.

When Jack and Clare woke up, it still appeared to be dark. They rose and pulled open the curtains. Dazzling sunshine filled the room. It was already noon. Clare saw a note by the side of the bed. She read:

Darlings, I'm off to the University, and from there, straight to the airport. So lovely seeing you both. Order breakfast and stay as long as you like!

Naomi x

'That must've been quite a lecture,' said Clare, as she laid back down on the bed in a shaft of warm light. She stretched and arched her naked body like a cat.

A grin spread across Jack's face. 'Well, she's quite a teacher.'

CONTROL

Thank fuck for that. Five past. That's all right, it won't have started yet. Now where the hell is he?

The steps to the opera house are empty. I can't even see much activity inside, just a load of staff in red tunics. He definitely said to wait out here. But Christ it's cold. You don't exactly buy Roland Mouret for its thermal qualities. Still, he won't be able to keep his hands off me when he shows his sorry self. Which suits me down to the ground. Who actually wants to watch opera anyway? I'll give it another minute out here then I'll...

My phone is ringing. It's Mark. He must be inside, in the warm. Bastard.

'Hello, where are you?'

'Sorry, babe,' he says. 'Bit tangled up at work. I... '

'You're still at work?' I realise I'm just holding the phone in front of my face and staring at it.

'The Swiss guys want the deal to go through tonight, so… '

'…you thought you'd just ignore the fact it's your girlfriend's birthday and the small matter that she's been standing out here, freezing her tits off for the last half an hour.' Okay, a small bit of artistic licence. But *really*.

'Look, Em,' he whines, 'you know I'll make it up to you. I always do. Be a good girl, enjoy the show and I'll see you at home afterwards.'

I'm guessing a little that that's what he said on account of the fact I'm once again holding the mobile in front of me, staring at it in disbelief. In despair. In a big fuck-off fury.

I scream into it, 'I only agreed to come to this bloody opera because of you, you little bastard. You gave me two hours' notice to get ready. Do you have any idea what I had to do to get here on time? Do you have any fucking idea? And don't "babe" me. It's my fucking birthday you little creep and you've ruined it.'

And with that I snapped my mobile shut. Not as satisfying as slamming a receiver down on a landline, but it made a decent enough crack in the silent, misty street, like a film clapperboard. And for a second I felt better. And not even cold.

I shouldn't be surprised. What's the point? He's done it before. He gives it all the 'well I only work the long hours for you, darling' but we both know that's a pile of crap. We could both live off my money – fuck, half of India could live off my money. But he won't do that. He's got a point to prove. It's all about rising up that ladder. And little Mark won't be happy until he's at the top of it so Daddy won't think he's such a disappointment.

Well, he's in for a rude awakening. Because he's got failure written right through him like 'Blackpool' through a stick of rock. But easier to fit in your mouth.

Suddenly it all boils over and I hear myself screaming alone into the darkness. I put it down to the cold – and the frustration. I had plans for the private box he'd booked – and they didn't involve watching overweight grotesques warbling sodding opera. As I'd carefully coated my lips on the way over, I'd visualised the scars my crimson lipstick would leave on his taut, pale body hours later, blood-red tattoos trailing down his neck, across his hairless chest and down, straight down to the bulging shorts beneath his suit. In fact, I'd got so excited about the idea in the cab ride over that I'd – but that's another story.

Then out of nowhere I hear a voice.

'Chin up, darling, plenty more fish in the sea!'

'Fuck off!'

My response is instinctive but I don't regret it. I can't even see who said it, but what's it got to do with him? Or anyone else for that matter.

'Come on, love, it can't be as bad as all that.'

There the voice goes again with its Christmas cracker philosophy. That's all I need. A wide boy with delusions of being Kilroy. Where is he anyway? And then I see him through the fog, across the road, a blond guy standing in the shadows beneath the neon sign of the club opposite. He's clad neck to toe in black. Shiny shoes, expensive looking long coat and a few bits of gold jewellery sticking out above the hands in his pockets.

'If you need someone to talk it through with, I'm only over here.'

What is this guy's fucking problem? Have I invited him to stick his oar in? I don't think so.

I look over at him again and he's holding out a cigarette. Lit. I haven't smoked since I was fourteen. But, Christ, it looks tempting right now. And suddenly I'm cold again. Maybe it wouldn't be the end of the world if I go over.

As I get closer, I see the distinctions in the black. There's been a lot of thought put into his outfit at some point. The heavy shoes, the clip-on tie, the light cotton shirt. It all points to him being ready for a bit of a scrap; nothing on him that could be used against him. Nothing that would actually hurt him if someone clung on. He's obviously a bouncer at this club, Nero's. And I'm going to talk to him! Jesus, what a birthday this is turning out to be.

'You always heckle strangers?' I ask as I approach. I need to put this guy in his place. Show him who's in control.

'Only the beautiful ones who look like they've been stood up.' Touché. I can't remember exactly what I said down the phone, but this hired heavy looks like he's worked it out all right.

'Must be one of the perks of being a doorman,' I suggest. 'You must see people like me dozens of times a night.'

He doesn't flinch at the obvious attempt to provoke flattery from him. Nor does he hand it over. What's his game? He's the one who summoned me. Shouldn't he be showing more interest?

'Listen,' he says, 'I couldn't help overhear you having a little problem with your man. And on your birthday too.' I glare at him. But he continues. 'Look, it's cold out here, why don't you come inside and let me buy you a drink?'

So that's it, that's his plan. Lure me over with the old 'buy you a drink' routine. What makes all men think they can solve everything with a drink? But why not? What have I got to lose by going in there with him? What's to stop me? I start to feel a flush of warmth as the excitement builds within me. Maybe I should. That would serve Mark right. Not that it was any of his business now.

'Well?' he says. 'I ain't got all night.'

I inhale the Marlboro Light and shake my head. 'I'll come in with you,' I say, 'but I'll buy my own drink.' He shrugs, but he opens the door and I walk past him and into the foyer of the club.

The first thing that hits me is the heat. The air conditioning machines directly above the door can't compete with this. There's only the ticket booth and the cloakroom up here, and the heat seems to have swirled its way up the dark, mirrored staircase, and wrapped its clammy hand around my entire body. From freezing a few moments earlier, I actually feel that now every inch of my skin is being bathed in sauna steam. My lipstick feels liquid on my lips; in my mind, the khol eyeliner threatens to join it.

The doorman gestures with his left hand and I head towards the stairwell. As I descend, I look in the mirror opposite and take a moment to study more closely my arrogant companion and tour guide. He has neat, short blond hair, an extremely clean shaven and angular jaw line that makes him look about twenty-five, although surely he's older? And twinkling eyes. I have no idea what colour they are, but they really do seem to be sparkling as he looks anywhere but at me as we go down. What is his problem?

The next thing that hits me, even before I reach the last step, is the noise. Deafening pulses of rhythm punctuating languid synthesiser sounds and soulful singing, each beat causing the mass of dancers in front of me to rise and fall as one. Arms sway in the air; they wrap around strangers' bodies; they hold drinks and cigarettes aloft. All the while, their bodies push closer together, lock closer together, writhe up and down, together.

I have never seen so many people squashed inside one room. It's not even half past eight and the place must already be sold out, twice over. Posters near me mention something about a forty-eight-hour 'week-ender'. Have these people really been here that long already? It smells like they might. The hot air that enveloped me upstairs is more intense down here, and I realise it's actually sweat. Pure fragrant perspiration. You can see it rising as steam from the mass of bodies on the dance floor. And I can smell it. Pure energy, pure passion, pure lust, mingling in the air, layering my body lightly like a spray-on tan. If I think about it tomorrow I'm sure I'll be disgusted. But right now, right here with the moisture of 1200 people's combined movements clinging to my skin, I think I like it.

I feel a firm hand on my elbow and it's him. His other hand directs me across the dance floor to where the bar must be. If he says anything, I can't hear it. He goes to lead but I ignore him and step forwards first.

For a second I falter. The giant wall of flesh in front of me seems to offer no entry. Faces enrapt in the music and in their partners, or potential partners, seem oblivious to anything outside their bodies' own movement. And what bodies. So toned, so dark, some tanned, some natural, the men's tight white vests raised high above their rippled midriffs or discarded once and for all. And the women's bikini tops and slinky braless dresses leave little to the imagination and less to chance. Strangers' hands sweep up and down each woman's curves, occasionally settling but never rejected. The women just turn, keep turning, admired by one face then the next, never making eye contact but never completely turning away. Under the guise of dancing they use their body as bait. It's primeval, as a woman I should be sickened. And yet I'm thrilled. I want to be a part of it, I want to enter that animalistic world, be torn apart by the baying pack. I want...

Once again the hand on my elbow, and I realise I have stopped walking. The doorman stands slightly in front of me, smiling, and slides his other hand between the backs of two gyrating clubbers. They yield slightly to his firm, cool touch and he beckons me forwards. The gap wouldn't fit a child, less a five foot ten woman, six foot in my red Manolo Blahniks, but I step into its shimmering maw and suddenly I'm among them. It's amazing. I can see faces, see mouths that mime the words to the song or lock onto the lips of another, I can see chests pressed against another's, backs rubbed against shoulders, legs entwined, but I can't see where they belong. I can't see any whole person. Everyone overlaps with everyone else. All the time still moving, still rising and sinking with the beat, but always reaching out and sharing space, sharing bodies.

In the opera house I know I would have stood out. Carefully pinned blonde hair piled strategically to make me look taller than I am, added to my most colourful – and bosomy – size ten frock, would have turned all the heads of the black tie geriatrics and City boys in there. The jealous whispers from their partners, all jewels and jowls, would only have inspired my haughtiness, would just have added to the exclusion zone around me. Beautiful. Untouchable. Me.

But here. Here I still stand out as a slash of colour on the darkened palette. But there is no exclusion zone, no air of mystery. I have entered their arena and I must play by their rules. If there are jealous whispers here, I can't make them out. I can't hear anything above the pounding basslines – anything, that is, except the cries of my body.

How many hands touch me as I walk slowly towards the bar? I lose count. Some land on my shoulders in avuncular concern for my safe passage. Others alight on my waist, one either side, in a silent, sexual request to dance. Some hands brush against my hips, or lower, one or two definitely stroking downwards across my bottom, others left to right across my Pilates-toned cheeks. Not threatening but persuasive, suggestive, and no one looking my way when I turn. And then – not a hand this time – almost certainly a kiss on the exposed part of my left breast from the shorter girl in dramatic makeup standing at my side. A strange power surges through me, reaches my pussy and spreads back to light up every inch of my skin. I look at the girl who has awakened me, she smiles, pokes out a studded tongue and turns away, lost in the waves of limbs.

Dazed, I reach the bar. Even though it stretches some thirty feet around the wall, the queue is at least four people deep and even outside the heaving throng, the music is as loud and there is no let up on the need to dance. I glance upwards at the array of spirits lining the mirror-backed shelves. Grey Goose, Belvedere, Zabrowksa. Perfect. And just to my right, high above the barmaids' heads, a panel of eight television screens, black and white, show different views of the action all around me. I can't see any cameras but I see me, even in monochrome, standing out. And behind me I see him, the blond hair inches from my own. He is not used to queuing in his club. I am not used to queuing anywhere. But tonight I make him. Because I can.

He leans in to say something to me and I feel his hot breath on my exposed, damp neck. If he says any words I don't hear them. The only communication I hear is from my pussy. What's this? A shiver runs along my arms, along my legs and, it really seems, even between them as well. Does he realise? Does he notice me tilt my head further away, pushing my neck closer to his mouth at the same time, encouraging him to speak silently to me further? I let my hand fall to my side and allow the back of it to brush against the doorman's groin. He does not flinch. And why should he? He is trained to stand his ground, to take on all-comers, to assert his authority and assume control.

But he is not in control now.

He moves his mouth against my neck and I feel his tongue slowly slide up, warm and soft, towards the back of my ear. I close my eyes, not daring to try to keep focused on the people around me. I'm. So. In. Control.

While his tongue reaches out, tasting the mix of perfume and the salt of a thousand people's lusty sweat, his nose nuzzles into the side of my head, pressing against the pinned up hair. And then – ouch! – he bites me. First gently on the bottom of my ear, a nip on the burning lobe. And then again, just below, on my neck, then again lower, and lower until I have a series of flashing burns running down to my shoulder.

My hand swings back at his trousers to tease him once more. But I can't. I mean to keep the back of my hand in contact, but his rigidity shocks me and I have to grab it. Fuck! So, so hard. His trousers are thick and tight, tighter than ever right now, and fixing a hold is difficult. But I reach down as low as I can without moving and sink my nails into the warm cloth, my thumb one side of his cock, my fingers the other, digging down towards his balls, and I grip. Keeping my hand still, I move my arm and feel the rub of his tip high against the back of my wrist. Left, right, left, right, I stroke slowly taking time to relay the feelings in my arm to my brain, never releasing my grip below, never letting his pleasure outweigh mine.

Still facing forward I feel his hand reach round my waist, the hardness in his trousers matched by the steely curve of his biceps. His other hand edges onto my arse, a full hand, fingers pointing to the floor, cupping my cheek and sinking his fingers into the flesh. His little finger clenches dangerously close to the crack between my legs, and even though it is some inches away, there is a pull on my pussy's lips as he squeezes. Fuck. Fuck. Fuck. That's good. So effortless, so instinctive. He's not even touching me there, but the more he gently kneads my cheek, the more my clit rubs against my silk panties, the more I moan. And the harder I grip.

He's standing right behind me now and my arm is reaching between us out of my own view, but I won't let go. Co-ordination is slow; everything is back to front so I have to focus to move left, really concentrate to squeeze up and push down. Left, right, up, down. Again and again.

His other hand fans out around my waist then edges up. The wire of my bra holds firm as his spreadeagled fingers trickle one at a time onto my uplifted but shuddering breasts. I'm perfectly in control, perfectly still, and it's as though they have a mind of their own, almost trembling with the rise and fall of each breath. He turns his wrist and rests the back of his hand on my left breast, his little finger darting below the dress line and flicking against my erect nipple. I lurch silently forward, my knees momentarily weaker. Then the finger emerges, and turned on its end, slowly scratches its nail along the pure white of my tremulous tits. Across one, then plunging into the narrow gap between them, then across the other. And back again, a thin raised red line appearing in the nail's wake as my skin responds.

All the while he licks and kisses and bites at my neck. All the while his right hand caresses my arse and bathes my clit in my own burning juices. All the while he groans, too low to be heard, they can only be felt as vibrations against my body.

For a second I'm aware of another hand on my waist, and the spell is broken. I open my eyes and see no one there, just anonymous faces, anonymous bodies, edging forwards, moving, dancing, pushing. And I see the screens again. I see us. I see the top of his head buried into the gentle curve of my nape. And I see his hand across my chest. Reaching now inside my bra, I feel him rolling my nipple between finger and thumb, gently at first, then pinching, then gently again. It's too good, too painful, too naughty – too much like his idea. Does he do this every night? Who is in control?

I don't care. His face on one of the screens above me is as clear as the scratches on my breasts. He could lose his job over this. And yet still he wants me. Still he needs to feel me pulling at him. Still he risks everything because of me.

Fuck, that hurt. Back in the moment again. My neck must have bites all over it. But I love it. It's pain like I've never felt before. The more my neck squeals, the more my pussy burns.

Working quickly, my right hand stops holding his cock and reaches up. His trousers are buttoned and I can slip a finger underneath the fold and between each stud. Oh, jeez. He doesn't wear shorts. I should have guessed, but I didn't, and my fingers are actually touching him. Right here, in the club, in front of hundreds of strangers.

It's too tight to get much of a grip but with one wrench, I feel several of the buttons release. How convenient. For both of us. I slowly reach into the opened gap and slide my nails for the first time across his balls, just like he does to my breasts, then drag them up against his hot, responsive cock, pulling it further into the fresh air as I go. For a few seconds I'm unaware of his left hand leaving my chest and sliding down to my hips. For a few seconds all I can think of is the thickness, the length and the leaking wetness of this fantastic cock that I've been stroking for five minutes without once seeing. And the not seeing is driving me mad.

Suddenly he lurches and I lose my grip. We're still pressed together, packed into an oblivious crowd, and I feel his hardness pressing against the top of my arse and above, skewering against my spine. He takes my hands in his and lowers them to my side, fixing them against the hem halfway up my thighs. Then reaching round behind me, down below his hardness, he holds the back of my £600 Galaxy dress – and rips. I don't hear it but I feel it. I feel the slight release of pressure against my cheeks, the loosening against my thighs. But mostly I feel his hands in direct contact with my buttocks, one finger, I don't know which, drawing a line up between the cheeks and hovering around the entrance. Then down again to the other, more welcoming, one and this time I have to respond. My entire body spasms forward and he reaches round with one arm to support me. With the other he steadies my back as he slowly lowers himself against me, until I feel it. I feel the hot, sticky film on his cock trace its way down against the coolness of my cheeks, lower, between my expectant thighs, then up, inside my flimsy silk knickers.

Then nothing. Stillness. Resting the tip of his cock against the fiery wetness of my cunt. The exchange of heat, the exchange of wetness, the exchange of questions between us. Do I want him to do this? Does he want to risk doing this? Can we get away with it? Do we care?

He kisses the back of my neck once more, places a firm hand on my left hip and pulls me back at the same time as he stands fully up.

Fuck fuck fuck fuck fuck.

I could not be more ready, but still that first sensation, that feeling of being stretched, of being violated, forced to take him in, screws me up inside. I can't think. I can't breathe. I can't stand.

I fall forwards, and although his arm around my waist catches me, my head rocks against the shoulder of the guy in front. He turns, smiles at the drunken partygoer behind him, and continues to dance. He has no idea of the cock sliding up inside me, filling me up, then pulling out, almost all the way so the air rasps around his cock and sends it plunging in again chilled. He has no idea of the strong hand reaching around the front of my dress and pressing through the fabric in a circular motion, then up then down, round and round, building slowly, building, building.

I feel like a rag doll shaken in a cat's mouth, a paper boat on the ocean, but I couldn't fall over even if I wanted to. The people pressing around me, their backs, their shoulders, their elbows and thighs, they keep me up with their movement. And it's knowing they're there, feeling their hot limbs against mine, sensing their eyes burning into my exposed cleavage and ravaged neck, that doubles the pleasure.

His hands are pressing just where I need to be pressed. His cock is filling me faster and faster, his bites getting harder and harder and… and…

God! Fucking God!

I scream at the top of my voice and damn anyone who hears me, anyone who cares that I've just come in their club. Oh my God, I feel weak, I feel hot, I feel drained, tired. But on fire. And dirty. I feel dirty, naughty, rude. And I like it.

And in control?

I feel his hands smoothing down the back of my dress, pulling the torn halves as close together as he can around the restored underwear. His hot juice, mixed with my own, trickles down my thigh, and for the first time I feel chilly. I wonder what I'd have to do to make him lend me his coat…

BELLADONNA

Italy, with its exquisite culture and even more exquisite men, draws me to her every spring. The long-awaited sun encourages clothes and Catholic constraints to be thrown off with equally careless abandon. Emerging from winter's hibernation away from hedonism, the Florentines' eyes stop blinking in the new light and fall again on the freshly exposed bodies of their fellow citizens.

Travelling always arouses my yearning for passion. The romance of exploring an undiscovered city unveils the tantalizing possibility of encountering a lustful partner – someone to revel in the blossoming season by indulging in carnal delights…

At the station I grab a map, a packet of cigarettes from the kiosk, and look for a taxi. The drivers are standing in a huddle, debating and gesticulating like a cartload of chimps. I am cool in comparison and their eyes all prey on me at once. A split-second silence and then an argument breaks out. Who will chauffeur me? I smile as the youngest and most striking of the group pushes his way manfully to my service.

It's a short drive to my hotel, but the silence is long. The ID card displayed on the dashboard tells me his name – Piero. His hazel eyes rest on my reflection in his rear-view mirror rather than on the buzzing traffic. I lower my eyes, playfully drawing his gaze to my low-cut cotton shirt, tied at the waist. My fuchsia laced bra teases him and almost causes an accident.

Under the pretence of re-tying my shirt, I loosen the knot, allowing my flawless stomach to be exposed for just a moment. Piero's eyes burn like lasers into the mirror and we swerve wildly across our lane. The rushing breeze through the half-open window hits my skin and my excitement starts to build... I feel aroused. Empowered. I don't care who sees me. I am on holiday, anonymous, carefree and spirited, and my desire for erotic adventures has no bounds.

I check in to my hotel and unpack. I enjoy a long luxuriant shower, and decide to raise the excitement stakes with a game of room service roulette. I time my order perfectly so that the knock on the door comes as I stand in the middle of my suite – naked and wet. The nearest cover is the white towelling dressing gown placed three feet away on the queen-sized bed. I call out 'Come in!' The gamble begins. How quickly can I get to the gown and cover myself? Will the waiter win by pushing the heavy door quickly enough to catch a glimpse of me? Or will he wrestle the door with his back? I move quickly, but not as quickly as I know I can. He turns into the room as I spin into the gown.

This intimate dance caught to the tune of one full breast left exposed, its perfect brown nipple still glistening from the shower, and a momentary flash of Brazilian strip. This waiter has seen a lot in his time but nothing as instant erection-inducing as this. Despite his olive skin, he blushes.

As I pay him his tip without bothering to tie the cord of my gown, I mischievously wonder whether instead he should have been paying me. Having got dry after my shower I am now happily wet between my legs once again.

It's late now so I'll savour room service for tomorrow morning's breakfast instead – so long as I'm back in time of course! I put on my clothes and go looking for a highly praised restaurant in the Oltrano district offered up by my guidebook. I decide upon a defiant black outfit for tonight which always provokes the right reaction – a tight black silk chiffon dress that exposes my sun-kissed arms and shoulders and barely hides my ample breasts… I delight in feeling ever so slightly naked.

I step outside the hotel in search of a drink and some fun. The streets of Florence are narrow and mysterious, looming residential doorways punctuated by the fluorescent glow of family-owned *ristoranti*. With my hotel map tucked tightly in my hand, I wander up and down the nocturnal streets, in search of the recommended establishment, slightly disorientated… I am sure that despite taking note of these same streets earlier on my journey to the hotel, I am now walking some remote and unfamiliar route.

I see a trio of young men coming towards me, strutting down the cobbled alleyway, laughing and shoving each other, high-spirited in preparation for their Friday evening.

As I approach, I take the opportunity to ask for directions to a bar. The atmosphere is still heavy and humid from the day's hot sun, and I am at least two drinks away from the sensation I desire.

'Scusi Signor, dove è una sbarra?'

They mutter something I do not understand as my school-learnt Italian fails me. I assume that they are intrigued by this creature before them wearing only a slip of a sundress which reveals my opulent breasts and some rather preposterously high sandals.

'Si Bella, over there.'

I turn to see where they are pointing and I can only see a door a little way up the street where a lantern is hanging.

Confused I give them a quizzical look. 'There?'

'Si, Si,' as the taller of the three outstretches his arm to indicate where I should go.

It's tempting to invite all three of them to join me, but instead I thank these young men and upon their Florentine recommendation stride resolutely to the bar.

I enter the dimly lit doorway and swing open the door which leads me to a dark corridor and some stairs. I can hear the faint sound of music as I find myself descending the winding stairwell, but even before I've reached the bottom the door moves ajar and I step through a corridor into a basement bar/club...

'Buena Sera, giovane donna.' An elderly gentleman nods his welcoming approval of my entry into this hidden saloon, and asks gently, 'Are you alone?'

My Italian is not as good as it used to be, but I understand his polite question and answer, 'Si, Si.'

I enter the darkened room that smells of cigarette smoke and am shown to a vacant table. My eyes adjust to the light and I can make out the dark silhouettes of amorous couples smoking and drinking with hands entwined and eyes fixed to the stage. I order a grappa and focus my attention on the lone man wearing what appears to be a top hat, and who is performing before the audience through the haze of smoke drifting up to the ceiling.

How intriguing to find myself sitting in this rather bizarre, intimate basement bar watching this magician run through a sequence of trickery and illusion. His hands dance lightly over a pack of cards, manoeuvring them from one hand to the other as if attached by invisible thread, and finally holding them aloft for examination. Leaning forward from the waist, his face in mock concentration, he scans the shadowy faces before him, deciding upon who to choose for his next act before settling on yours truly. Is he a psychic as well as a magician? Does he sense that I will be a willing assistant for him?

Accepting his hand to guide me up the small step onto the tiny stage, he positions me so I am standing close to him, so close in fact I can feel the heat of his skin. His hand brushes mine as he procures the pack for me to choose a card... this gives me the opportunity to examine his handsome features. He smiles warmly at me with a full sensuous mouth that I would happily like to explore and dark, mesmerizing eyes. I scan the length of his athletic build as he proceeds with engaging the audience with the finale of the trick. I imagine he is inviting me into his fantasy world. Caressing my breasts, stroking my inner thigh with his magic wand. The crescendo of the trick reaches its conclusion with audible gasps and apprecia-tive claps. Having played my part, I bow to the audi-ence, wink at the magician and gracefully find my seat to enjoy his performance and order a stiff drink.

At the end of the show the *conjuror* receives an encore, with the stage light illuminating not only his lone figure on the stage, but the audience too. This gives me a chance to make meaningful eye contact with several young gentlemen, whom I hope my approving gaze might entice to my table.

'Ciao, Bella…'

I turn to look straight into the eyes of the delicious magician. 'May I join you?'

Without much hesitation I indicate my assent, and he signals to the waiter to bring, I'm guessing, some more drinks for us to enjoy. He certainly is beautiful without his top hat obscuring his features. His hair is longer than I had realised and falls in soft dark curls around his ears, complimenting his masculine jaw and angled cheekbones. He has the looks of a man who might inspire Da Vinci to sketch in nude or Donatello to carve an imitative statue.

A bottle of red wine arrives and he pours it into two large glasses.

'Thank you for being my gorgeous assistant tonight,' he says.

His smooth hand reaches out and touches my face. I breathe in the faint scent of his skin, intoxicated by this handsome stranger. I feel, with surprised delight, the moisture building between my legs. I am ready. I want to be exploding on his cock. I want him so badly, just for him to touch my skin, move his hand up my skirt, stroke the soft flesh of my thigh. When will he push the damp fabric of my knickers aside, two fingers deep in my pussy, feeling the wetness, with his thumb circling my clit? Deliberate in my moves, my left hand falls to rest on his muscular thigh, his cock shifting slightly in his trousers.

I take a sip of the Chianti and my face flushes. At this point, I whisper that I am not feeling too well and rise to find the bathroom. I pause at the door and glance back, I see my magician turning in his seat, searching my body language for a signal.

I shut the door. With the excitement of the unexpected cabaret, I have forgotten all about the restarant and food. I am intoxicated by both the alcohol and my magical encounter. I splash water onto my face. Turning off the tap I swing round and almost collide with someone else who has entered the bathroom whilst I have been bent over the sink. It takes me a few seconds to recognise that it is the sexy illusionist. Deft of hand he locks the door, signalling that the time for illusions has finished. He kisses me – hard and urgent.

My whole body pulsates as our mouths connect. I smile at him and grind my hot pussy into his belly as he lifts me onto the edge of the basin. My breasts press hard against his chest and my hands reach to feel his taut buttocks. I pull him closer. There is an animal-like ferocity to our bathroom liaison.

I feel my clit pulsing at the excitement of his touch… I want him to fuck me so *hard*, to feel him deep inside me, teasingly rubbing the head of his cock around the outside of my opening before dipping into my juices and doing me hard from behind.

He turns me around to face the mirror, and I offer no resistance. I watch as his hand slips under the sheer fabric of my dress to reach the outer boundaries of my underwear. His dexterous fingers explore the edge of lace and urgently release my tits which spill out of their constraints. He circles my nipples and they transform into hardened tips beneath his masterful touch. I turn and rub my generous cleavage across his face. His hands are soft, tracing all the way down the curve of my stomach to the top of my knickers – long since moistened with all this attention.

He grabs my shoulders and pushes me to the ground. His hand closes into a fistful of my auburn hair as he guides me gently downwards, level to the constrained pleasure of his cock as he lets out a sigh of anticipation.

I too am excited and hungrily trace my fingers across his loins and struggle to release him from his black trousers.

It's everything I had wished for. I oblige him by leaning forward with parted lips and my tongue gently flicks across the top of his cock. With an odd tenderness I study his penis, smile and then take the full length of him into my mouth, all the way to the base. My tongue slides deliciously up the length of his cock as he lets out an insistent moan. I suck hard as he penetrates my throat, gorging greedily, feeling my cunt contracting with every downward swoop of my mouth. I change tempo slightly, stroking and licking him and his balls tighten. I tilt my head back to see if he is watching, knowing that he will be. My mouth around his hard cock drives his excitement further. There are no rules and no boundaries

'Come here, Bella. I want to…' he growls, urgency in his voice.

His hands are on my shoulders now, lifting me, and I slide up his body and slip my tongue into his mouth… forcing him to taste his own sex.

He swivels me round, one hand on my waist, the other between my legs, his fingers nudging my swollen clit. I am excited not only by the thrill of this guy but also the delicious possibility of us getting caught. He breathes hard, fighting for control. With my skirt pushed high and my cunt lips desperately wanting to be filled with him, he plunges his cock into my aching hole and starts thrusting hard against my buttocks. We grind together harder and harder, my arched back rising up to meet his deep, quickening thrusts. God I'm so close now – my hands grip the basin and I catch a glimpse of him in the mirror, his face obscured by a mass of dark curls. I know I am helpless as I feel the irresistible sensation of orgasm rising within me.

I am so close to coming…my breath has transformed into short gasps of pleasure… his hand is rhythmically stroking my clit while he pounds into me, my excitement heightening. I cry out until I feel the first pulse of orgasm, his cock pushing right through me, both of us reeling, spilling over, emptying ourselves of our lust.

As the heat subsides, we collapse forward, his arm loosely around my waist, and he kisses my neck.

I straighten my clothing, turn and face him and we embrace in a long tender kiss. I unlock the door and move through the bar. Opening my clutch bag, I leave a fistful of euros on the table and swiftly sashay through the tables. I leave how I entered – never looking back.

The next day, it is hot and beautiful and I am wandering around the famous monuments and statues. I look up and am face to face with the most perfect of men; my gaze falls to his naked form and I smile sweetly to myself, as I am reminded of my Florentine encounter. Michelangelo's *David* has a glorious Italian penis just like my magnificent magician.

YOUR FRIENDS AND NEIGHBOURS

He stood in the corridor. He listened for sounds coming from inside the room. But she was silent. No sound came. He stared at the ceiling and waited. He wanted her to complain, to moan, to *something*, but she resisted. Maybe she was asleep behind that door, or maybe she was holding her breath. He had said he'd be back over half an hour ago. But still he made her wait.

The room had an echo. She knew it was small and she knew it was empty. Other than the wooden seat that splintered underneath her, she assumed there was another seat across the table from her. Maybe another two. That was normal. The handcuffs that bit into her skin were threaded between the leg of a metal table.

She knew that it was bolted to the floor, because she had already tried to run her hands down the smooth leg to see if she could lift the table and remove her arms. She was stuck here. That much was clear. And she hadn't heard anything other than the sound of her muffled breathing for quite some time now. She had begun to count the seconds. *One Mississippi, two Mississippi*... It was the only way to stop her screaming out for someone to come. But she'd been here before. She wasn't going to give anyone the satisfaction of a scream. She could wait. This wasn't the first time she'd been left in a room, handcuffed and blindfolded.

He checked his watch. It had been an hour and forty-five minutes. She must be thirsty in there. Sufficiently confused. He knew he'd like this one. He knew he had her all to himself. So he made her wait long enough to be grateful for his arrival. It didn't matter who he was. After two hours alone, she'd be grateful.

Could she hear something? Was he waiting by the door? There was definitely some movement out there. The regular *huff... hurr* breathing of her mouth had been joined by another sound. The air had shifted. She could hear rustling by the door. He was there. Listening. She held her breath. Sucked in the droplets of perspiration that rested on the brow of her lip. Didn't want him to see her anything other than composed.

Two hours. He unlocked the door loud and fast hoping to make her jump. She didn't move. Her thin arms lay in a relaxed supplicated pose on her knees, her palms upwards. Her shoulders were pulled back as if she were trying to maintain some kind of posture, despite the fact that her torso, because of the cuffs, was leaning in at a severe angle. The blindfold was tight against her face, so tight that her flesh pressed over the edges of it. He couldn't make out how her hair usually looked, bunched up as it was in the knot. He glanced over the taut terrain of her body. *Yes*. Her cleavage tried to hide itself between her upper arms but it peeked out over her ripped shirt. *Beautiful*, he thought, and scanned her legs.

He was checking her out. She knew this from his silence. She waited for him to get his fill. She pressed her wrists together to make her breasts stand out more. His footsteps came closer. They were heavy. A brief flicker of panic flooded her bloodstream. She had been expecting a lighter man, a smaller man, but this man sounded big. Heavy. She tried to control her heartbeat. Let the panic leave. Why should she be more afraid of a heavier man? *Small men are even more dangerous*, she told herself. *Small men are ones without conscious. Big men don't want to hurt you just because they feel inadequate. Good that he is big. There is more chance of me getting out alive.*

He stood behind her. He wanted the first time she heard his voice to be from behind, to be all the more disorientating.

'This shouldn't have been done to you. It's not normal procedure.'

'I know.'

'Are you a lawyer?'

'No.'

'Then how do you know about procedure?'

'I've been here before.'

'And?'

'And I was never blindfolded before.'

'Would you like me to remove it?'

A pause. Why was she hesitating? Did she think it was a trick? He hoped she thought it was a trick.

'If– If you don't have a problem removing it… that would be preferable.'

'That's fine,' he said, and wound his fingers round the knot and yanked it off. Her hair tumbled out in a cascade of dirty brown ringlets behind her.

The light burned into her eyes. She immediately had to close them. *Damn!* She had instinctively reached up to rub them and only succeeded in cutting her wrists still deeper on the cuffs. She shook her head, face down towards her waist, her eyes screwed shut. 'Is there any way you could… dim the lights or something?'

'There's only one setting for the lights I'm afraid. I could put the blindfold back on.'

She slowly blinked open her eyes. She had been right about the room. It was a sterile-looking cube with a thin film of dust glossing the vinyl floor. The table was bolted down, but only big enough to hold two cups of coffee maybe, or a dinner for one, nothing more. There was no chair opposite her. Why he stood behind her, she didn't know. She didn't crane to see him. He would show himself soon enough. But she noticed something that made her nervous. She decided to play nice. This was not the time to be a wiseass.

'You look concerned.' He stepped in front of her. Allowed her to take in his frame, his build, his suit. Her frown remained fixed as her eyes, still squinting, looked over his body. He wondered what she was making of him. Big man like himself. She probably hadn't had the pleasure of such an imposing specimen in some time. Too busy hanging out with radicals who, in his vast experience, were always short, hairy and skinny. 'What's the matter?'

She wondered if, by voicing it, she might make things more dangerous for herself. She didn't want to say anything that might set him off. But on the other hand, she had rights. She steeled herself. 'There's no mirror in here.'

'So?'

'Well...'

'You look fine to me,' he said.

'But it means... no one's watching us.'

He slowly took off his jacket, like a boxer removing his gown at the start of a fight. He leaned on the table. His forearms bulged against his shirt sleeves. He looked pleased with himself. There was a confidence in his eyes. A small smirk on his lips. Unwatched, he could do what he wanted with her and no one would be any the wiser.

'Would you like to be watched?' he said, and she hated him for saying that, for the way he said it, for the fact that she knew eventually the talking would stop. And when it did, handcuffed as she was, she would have no chance at controlling the situation.

When she raised her face to his, he felt himself flinch from her stare. Her eyes were blue, steely blue, sensually blue, burning blue right into his own. The eye contact made him feel naked. He stood up straight again. Tried to ignore the sensuous shape of her lips. The way they seemed permanently on the verge of saying, 'Oh...' Back to business.

'Do you know why you're here?'

'Not really.'

'What does that mean?'

'I have an idea. But it's not true.'

'What's not true?'

He had begun to pace in front of her, trying to regain his assertion of the room by marking out more territory within it.

'I didn't kill him.'

'No?'

'No.'

'But you were found with him.'

'Yes.'

'You were naked.'

'Yes.'

'In fact, you were both naked, weren't you?'

'Yes. We were.'

'And yet, you didn't call the police. Nothing. You just happened to be lying naked next to a naked dead man.'

'I didn't just *happen* to be there.'

'Were you the deceased's wife?'

'No.'

'But you are married?'

'Yes.'

'So you were cheating on your husband?'

'Where's my lawyer?'

'There's no lawyer coming.'

'I know my rights.'

'What rights?'

'I can choose not to talk to the police until my lawyer is present.'

He forced himself back to the table, to level his eyes with hers.

'Who says I'm the police?'

Her heart dropped a notch or two, like she'd been punched in the gut. If he wasn't the police, who the hell was he? And what was she supposed to do now? She forced a half-smile onto her face. Looked at him seductively.

'Please…'

'What?'

'Please undo the handcuffs. I won't go anywhere.'

She let him look at her. His eyes ran over her again, glancing at her wrists then slowly down over the smooth curves of her legs. He moved his eyes back to hers.

'I won't let you leave.'

'I won't try.'

He moved towards her. Knelt down next to her. His hair stroked her cheek as he leaned his head down towards her hands.

Being this close to her, he could feel her heat, the beat of her heart that emanated through her pores. The smell of her. The fresh salty smell of her skin. He breathed it in. Wanted to touch her. And maybe give her the gentle treatment. But he shouldn't. He had a job to do. He slipped the key into the grooves and unlocked the cuffs with a clink.

But instead of continuing the interrogation, he did something unexpected. He took her wrists in each of his hands and gently rubbed them with his fingers, like a father might with their child. She smiled instinctively. She felt safe. Why had she been afraid of him? And now, with him knelt towards her, she knew it would all be OK. She gently scraped her chair backwards.

Before he knew what had happened, her knee was in his chest and he was flat on his back, the chair toppling over next to him. His head clocked the floor with surprising force and he let out an involuntary oof! He didn't have time to process how fast her reflexes had been but now she was straddling him, her knees pinning his elbows, her face looming down towards him. She stared him in the face, a small pendulum motion side to side with her neck, like a cat surveying its prey.

'Two hours?' she said, with barely contained rage. '*Two hours!*' She slapped him hard across the cheek, and then repeated the phrase, beating him about the chest. He struggled to move his arms – she really had him pinned – and he was finding it hard to breathe as her fists rained down on him. 'Two fucking hours you leave me in here!'

Her heart was thumping in her chest. Her veins were engorged with blood. She looked down at the man. It felt good with him underneath her. She liked the look of fear on his face. 'I'm sorry,' he was mumbling, 'I thought, I just...' She flew in with her face to his again, her nose centimetres from his.

'You just what?'

He stared up at her and she knew she had him. He wanted her.

'I just wanted answers.'

'I don't want to give you answers.'

She sat up. Stared him down. 'But I'll *show* you what happened.'

She leaned off him carefully, aware that letting him go could lead to trouble. She grabbed the cuffs from the floor and brought them near to him.

'I'm going to release your arms,' she said. 'And when I do I want you to raise them above your head. OK?' She put her lips close to his, aware that the only way to keep him in order was through eye contact. 'OK...' he uttered nervously. She slipped her knees off his arms, holding his gaze with hers. Slowly, he moved his arms up, past her waist, his fingers brushing her arse, past her torso, sliding past the side of her breasts and over his head. She threw a quick glance up and raised the cuffs. She hooked them together, his wrists crossed. 'Now you're going to be a good boy, aren't you?'

'Yes,' he swallowed.

He was completely at her mercy. She sat on top

of him, this alpha lioness, this feverish feline, her mascara-streaked face, her wild eyes, her defined body and this wicked smile – she could do what she wanted; he was essentially fucked, his career ruined, no escape and all he could really think was *I am the luckiest man alive*. She stood up over him, her feet on either side of his waist. He tried to lift his head to get a glimpse under her skirt. 'Don't fucking move.' She raised her hand as if to calm him. He obeyed. She inhaled deeply as if it was the first smoke of the day. And then released the breath in a small plume.

'He wanted me to dance for him. See, my husband, he doesn't like the chase anymore. Doesn't have the patience for it. Just likes to fuck me from behind and then go to sleep. But with this man… He liked to watch me. Take it all in. Prolong the moment. Prolonged it so much it killed him. He liked me to do this…' She got down on to her haunches. Her arse stretched though her skirt. She brought it on top of his waist. Let it rest just above his cock. Swayed a little. Let the air between her behind and his front warm up. Let it raise the temperature. And all the time she never broke eye contact. It was killing him too.

She unzipped his suit trousers. His cock was already erect, pressed against his thigh. She freed it and brought it out into the open. It screamed out to her, and she gave it a squeeze, one firm hold, then let it go again. She brought her face back to his. 'Kiss me,' she said. He was sweating, red, breathless. He raised his head. She forced it back onto the floor, her fingers twisting in the roots of his hair. And then her tongue was in his mouth and he breathed heavily through his nose, and beneath her she could feel the twitching of his cock, as it groped upwards, trying to connect to a part of her, any part of her.

She wouldn't break the kiss. He thought he might suffocate under the relentless, joyous assault of her lips and tongue and spit that enveloped and consumed his. He opened his eyes. Caught a glimpse of hers. They were closed, and he loved that. And his cock was trying to escape from his body, to go rogue, to have freedom, it needed to be touched! He wanted his hands out of the cuffs, not to do anything other than grab himself and be released from this torture.

And then as if she had read his mind, she reached down and grabbed it again. With her other hand she lifted her skirt and he smiled to know she had no panties on, and she forced him inside her and it fitted so snugly, so smoothly, just glided right in, she was so wet and when she lowered herself fully on to him, his cock pushed through her, deep inside, enveloped itself inside her, and she clung on as she rode him, her hands splayed against his chest and she balanced herself on him like a dancer on a music box and she pushed herself further on to him, pushed down harder until she felt she was so completely full with his cock that his cock was now the space on the earth that her body once occupied; and she wanted him to reach for her breasts, but his hands were cuffed so she pressed them together herself, pushed down on her erect nipples, tried to bury them inside her own flesh and she watched his eyes squinting along with the crease of his mouth as he let out the strangled *urgrghhhs* of his ecstasy and she ground into him, she was nearly there, she was right on the edge, ready to fall, ready to die, and she pushed one more time and all her muscles contracted as she felt the hot gush of his come as it shot through her. She squeezed his cock to keep him hard, she wasn't ready to stop yet and she rubbed her pubic bone against his, and her whole body blushed, a deep bloom that spread from her breasts down to her ankles and her calves and her thighs and her abdominals and all the muscles in her body, *everything*, tensed and relaxed, tensed and relaxed for a good twenty seconds until she was nothing but a shaking mass on top of this man. She closed her eyes. Her mouth was open. Hot gasps of breath escaped from her lungs. She took a minute to bring herself back inside her head and then reached over and undid his cuffs. He reached up automatically and put his arms round her. She let herself be held, one palm on her hair, the other on her shoulder.

She lay full weight on him as he stroked her back.

He felt empty. Breathless. He wanted to cry. He rubbed her shoulder hard, tried to get rid of the feeling. She moaned softly.

'I… I don't want to do it anymore. I… I don't like hurting you.'

She looked upwards at his face. She smiled and ran her finger over his cheek.

'You never hurt me.'

'I feel like I could…'

'It's OK. I still love you.'

She kissed his fingers one by one.

And she wondered where they would meet next time. And what role she would have to play. She knew there would be a next time. There always was. One day they would have to stop this. One day they would have to join the rest of the world. Go on dates. Meet for drinks. Go to the theatre. Settle down. Take care of other people. Have dinner parties. Take a passing interest in politics. Learn yoga. Follow recipes by celebrity chefs. Go to the countryside for weekend breaks. Get an early night to beat the morning rush. Have phone conversations that end with, 'See you later,' instead of, 'I'll be waiting…' He had sworn that one day they would be normal. In fact, he said they had no choice. She thought about it while his fingers languidly combed through her hair. Maybe after the next time…

THE SECRET

Tom threw his Burberry raincoat over his shoulder and, with a faint smile, turned and headed down the long bright corridor toward the penthouse door.

Rachel stood and watched him go, pulling the silk kimono closer round her naked shoulders.

'I hope I haven't made you too late,' she said to his retreating form.

He blew a kiss, smiled again and was gone.

Rachel stood for a moment and stared at the door. She could still taste him in her mouth. And she could hardly believe what she was going to do later today. She sighed deeply, turned and walked languidly into the sitting room. She pushed a small button on the wall and the curtains silently slid back to reveal the floor-to-ceiling penthouse windows. She contemplated the vista below, the pre-dawn lights of the city twinkling in the distance. Few people were stirring as far as she could see, and as she took in the other towering city apartment buildings and low-rise flats of the central district, Rachel wondered how many other women had made love this early in the day. Or been so passionate. Or felt so guilty.

She caught sight of her reflection in the window and opened her kimono to expose her body. She wasn't worried about anyone seeing her. Her breasts were firm and she turned sideways to inspect her long legs and flat belly. Tom liked her belly. Rachel had found this a bit strange at first. She knew there were boob men, or arse men or leg men, but she'd never heard of a belly man. Although in truth, it was almost the first thing Tom had seen of her. They'd met at a photoshoot for beachwear at a studio in Soho. Advertisers seemed to like her traditional blonde hair... Tom was modelling swimwear too, although he was the art director and had only decided to model when one of the other guys failed to show up. Rachel was quite glad the photographer persuaded Tom to stand in. It was obvious he worked out, although it wasn't actually Tom's bulging biceps or glistening six pack or even – let's face it – the straining swimming trunks that first caught Rachel's attention. It was actually his eyes. Then the trunks. But first, his eyes. Deep, piercing grey eyes. Maybe they were destined to be together forever. The Belly Man and The Eye Girl!

They married a year after that first shoot and they now boasted six very happy years together. She loved him passionately and he loved her passionately. Although he had been surprised at the level of her passion at five o'clock this morning.

But she had a guilty secret. And when she awoke early and stared at Tom's gently sleeping form in the dim light of the bedside clock, she needed to assuage her guilt somehow. And one way to ease her guilt was to pleasure her husband. So she reached out and stroked his shoulder outside the sheet. She slid her hand down his back and over his firm buttocks and caressed him between his legs. He moaned and turned onto his back and she threw back the sheet and as he slipped from sleep she kissed his chest and his stomach and down until he was swelling in her mouth. And she licked and sucked and cupped him awake. He soon came and she eagerly devoured him. She was hazy and musty with love, but still her guilt was not washed away.

Tom smiled and showered and kissed her and threw his raincoat over his shoulder and left for work a happy man with a great life and a great wife. But Rachel wanted to selflessly sex him because she knew that the next time she saw Tom, when he came back from the agency tonight, she would have betrayed him. She had been completely faithful for all their six years together, but today was the day that Rachel was going to fuck another man. And what was even stranger was she didn't even know his name.

It was Tom's fault really, she supposed. He hadn't done anything specific to drive her into the arms of another man, but that was the problem. He hadn't done anything at all – except work. She hardly saw him. He left the apartment early and returned late. It had been the same every day since they came to Manchester. It was a big promotion for Tom, establishing a new ad agency in the city and the contract was only for three years. But Rachel had left a full life in London and up here she knew nobody. Financially the job was a dream. But all the money in the world couldn't make up for the isolation she was feeling. In Notting Hill she had been an active member of the local health club and lunched regularly with her friends at some of the smaller, more intimate bistros on Portobello Road. Here she knew nobody and although Manchester boasted some fine restaurants, who would she go with? She hated the term 'bored housewife'. It was such a stereotype. But she couldn't help feeling that her life was... well, frankly boring. And her best friend, Lucy, was not helping. Lucy was still in London and they spoke or e-mailed every day. Lucy had instantly suggested that one way to bring a little excitement into her life was to have an affair. Rachel had dismissed the idea. She loved Tom and the thought of betraying him was too terrible to consider. So she forgot Lucy's advice and tried to make the best of what she currently had. She spent many hours and many thousands of pounds trawling through some of the best shops in the city. She joined the local gym, one of the most exclusive in town. And she began to explore the network of picturesque canals running through the city. But it was still not enough. She could distract herself for a while, but ultimately her boredom returned. Her life began to feel hollow, almost meaningless. It was perhaps because she had so much time on her hands that she turned more and more to sex. She looked at porn on the Internet and ordered a new vibrator. She would go to the gym on Monday, Wednesday and Friday, but on the other days she would wander around the apartment, often naked, and indulge in the vibrator. She used different rooms and tried different positions. It seemed anytime she was on her own, she would masturbate and she included every room of the new apartment in her orgasmic fantasies. Once, she even opened one of the penthouse windows to the balcony and sat outside, naked, with the vibrator and bought herself to a climax, thrilling at the fact she may be seen by anyone. And as she masturbated more often, her fantasies became wilder.

When they had first moved to their new apartment they'd had a problem with a light switch. An electrician had been called. He was a handsome man, but Rachel had taken little notice of him at the time. However now she began to include him in her fantasies. He would call to fix some electrical fault and ask for payment. She would find herself without money. He would be sympathetic, but insist on payment. So she would pay him with her body. Her fantasies became more elaborate. There would be other problems in the apartment. A leaking tap. She called a plumber. A crack in the plaster. She called a builder. The builder brought a young apprentice with him. Each time Rachel was without money and paid with her body, letting them take her however they wanted. The fantasy callers became ever more demanding. They would sometimes insist on tying her to the bed before plunging into her. They'd demand she shout or swear as they came. Then her invented Lotharios occasionally became voluptuous, sweet-smelling girls. But they would also be demanding, and strip her gently before burying their tongues inside her. And she began fantasising about a man she'd seen once at the gym. He was about six feet tall, with a shock of jet-black hair and a strong jaw. His eyes were a steely blue – God, how she loved those eyes – and he must have been in his early thirties. His chest was toned but not muscle-bound and he had well-formed thighs and calves. He was quite beautiful, in a smouldering way. Her imagination added any missing details. She never saw him again at the gym, but in her mind he began visiting her regularly. She didn't know his name so she made one up for him. She decided he would be called 'Oliver'. She liked that name.

Rachel started to worry that her sexual obsession was becoming all-encompassing. She decided to go back to some of the classic books she'd not read for a long time. The first book she came to on the shelf was *Lady Chatterley's Lover*. She'd been looking for the literary equivalent of a cold shower and this most definitely was not it. But it was a great read and she began to devour it.

She also tried long walks. It was on one of her walks by the canal that she noticed a sign for a cycle route and it gave her an idea. She'd read an article in one of her style magazines that cycling was becoming the new horse riding. The piece may have been a fiction, but she decided to check out bicycles on the Internet and sure enough, she found a wide array of luxury bikes for women. She decided it would be a healthy way of getting around and it was something she could do to amuse herself without drawing attention to her loneliness. And when the summer arrived she could check out more of the canal towpaths and explore her new city. She mentioned her plans to Tom one night when he eventually came to bed. He simply grunted his approval and fell asleep.

Rachel found a specialist bike shop nearby, in the city centre. She walked to the shop one afternoon, having spent most of the morning with the vibrator and a small army of handymen and handywomen and Oliver from the gym. He had been most demanding!

She walked in to the modern, double-fronted shop, crammed with bikes and accessories. She asked the young assistant for advice on the type of bike she should buy. As he went to the back of the shop to fetch a catalogue for her, Rachel froze. Standing just in front of her was 'Oliver' in the flesh. Rachel felt a tremor of excitement as he turned and walked past her toward the entrance. Their eyes met, briefly, and he gave a little smile, then was gone. Rachel stood for a moment, rooted to the spot. It was only the second time she had seen him in real life, but in her mind they had done the most intimate things.

Rachel bought a bike and, fairly successfully pushing naughty thoughts of Oliver out of her mind, rode home with a new lease of energy, relishing the sense of freedom. But as soon as she arrived back at the apartment she threw herself onto the bed, half-flushed with the bike ride and half-flushed with thoughts of the man in the bike shop. His face, she thought, was exactly as she had remembered it. A strong, square jaw. High cheekbones for a man, and those piercing, ice-blue eyes. Her dark and beautiful stranger. She wondered what he did. Perhaps he was a plumber. Or a gamekeeper! Rachel laughed out loud as she reached for the book on the bedside table. Of course, she thought. His name is Oliver Mellors and I'm the Lady who will employ him! She read *Lady Chatterley* for a little while longer, but soon dozed off and dreamt of wild passion with rough country men.

Rachel didn't really believe in fate, but it was an incredible coincidence that after seeing him in the bike shop, almost every time she went out after their first, fleeting glances, it seemed she saw her mystery man. Again at the gym. Then walking out of a wine bar. Then again in her local shopping mall. Mostly he was unaware of her, although if their eyes did meet, he would always smile.

It was ironic that as Tom seemed to become more remote, she was building a relationship with a man she had never even spoken to. She used the man in her fantasies, but in reality she felt even more isolated. Although her mood was darkening, the weather was not. So she decided to get out and enjoy the sunshine. On one of her bike rides, she'd noticed that a quiet meadow ran along by the canal. She decided it was the perfect location to banish her dark mood with a little light reading. Lady Chatterley and Mellors were to be her companions.

She found a bench and settled down with the book. It was the peace of the place that appealed to her, the canal before her reflecting a shimmering sun in a crystal blue sky. Although near the middle of a major city, there was total silence, save the humming of insects and the whisper of the trees. She hoisted her dress up a little further to allow her legs to catch the sun,

She read for a while, then sighed and looked up, feeling warm and relaxed. In the distance, a figure on a bike was riding toward her. She realised she'd been here for nearly an hour without seeing another soul. She glanced back at the rider and suddenly her heart seemed to skip a beat. It was Oliver. She could hardly believe it. Here, in the glorious isolation of the meadow, was her Oliver.

Rachel ruffled her dress back down to cover her legs and pretended to read. She could hear him approaching. She waited for him to pass but he stopped. Her insides turned somersaults as he sat down next to her. She stared at the book without really reading and felt, rather than saw, his presence.

'We meet again,' he said, in a soft Scottish burr.

Rachel realised she had been holding her breath. She looked around at him in a fluster.

'Er… me? Again? Oh yes… I see… yes. Hello there. At the gym…'

'…and the bike shop. Nice bike, by the way.'

'Oh yes. Er… thank you.'

'Sorry to intrude – I'm Oliver.' He extended his hand with a beguiling ease. 'I'm new round here.'

'What!' Rachel could hardly speak. 'Oliver. Hi. I'm… Constance. Er… Connie,' she said, hiding the book. 'I'm quite new here too.'

She took his hand and shook it. The grip was soft but firm. She had no idea why she would lie about her name. Or maybe she did!

The next half hour passed in a haze for Rachel. She was beguiled but confused by her familiar stranger. He told her he was from Edinburgh, working on a project in town. She couldn't remember later what the project was, but it didn't seem to matter. It was finished anyway, which would explain why Rachel had seen more of him recently. They talked about the bikes. This was his first bike since childhood. They talked about Manchester and about Notting Hill – it turned out he'd spent some time working on the Brompton Road. But although the conversation was free and easy, neither asked or gave away any personal information. Neither asked about marriage or partners. And it was slowly dawning on Rachel that she preferred it that way. Indeed, it was a shock when Oliver told her he only had two days before he would have to return to Edinburgh.

'Oh, you're going that soon, are you?' she said, hoping he wouldn't pick up the faint hint of disappointment in her voice.

'Afraid so,' he said. 'And it's real shame. Just as I've discovered the most beautiful thing in Manchester.' She could feel the colour rising in her cheeks. 'I'm talking about you'.

'Oh,' she smiled. She felt like a schoolgirl again. She hoped he wouldn't notice her blushing. 'Well, thank you.'

'Look, I know we've only just met. But could we meet again tomorrow? Maybe here? I'll bring a picnic if it's nice.'

'Um... well...,' she didn't want to appear too keen. 'A picnic,' she smiled. 'That's very old fashioned!'

'Traditional.' He said. 'The best way to eat, Connie.'

Connie? Oh yes. Constance. Her.

'We could go to the bistro if you'd prefer that.'

'No, here would be just fine. Shall we say one o'clock?'

'Perfect.'

He leaned over and gave her a peck on the cheek.

'See you at one tomorrow, then.'

She watched him cycle off. He was very fit. She felt a mixture of thrilling excitement and terrible fear. Although she hadn't made her mind up, she thought she knew exactly where this was going to end.

That night, Tom was again unresponsive, but in one way, Rachel was pleased. It helped her out of her moral dichotomy. So she was resolved. She would simply encourage Oliver and see what happened. She had nothing to lose, particularly as Oliver would be gone forever… soon.

The following day, Rachel awoke with a feeling of guilty anticipation. Pleasuring Tom had not eased the guilt, nor had it changed her mind. She prepared for her big adventure. She donned her most provocative underwear, a short skirt and a figure-hugging top. Before she left she checked herself in the mirror. She looked good and left the apartment feeling confident and brave.

She arrived at their agreed spot ten minutes early and, sure enough, Oliver appeared on time, carrying a wicker basket. With a smile, he sat down next to her.

'Hi. Thought I'd better leave the bike today. They're not built for carrying picnic hampers.'

She smiled as he opened the hamper.

'I'm not really sure what you like, so I had them make up a bit of everything. There's fois gras, smoked salmon…'

'Had *them* make up a bit of everything?' interrupted Rachel. 'Who are *they*?'

'Oh, the hotel.' He laughed. 'You don't think I bring a picnic hamper from Edinburgh on all my jobs do you?'

'I suppose it depends on how many picnics you arrange with strange women…,' said Rachel, with just a hint of a smile.

'Never done it before. And anyway, don't knock yourself, you're not that strange.'

'Why thank you, kind sir,' Rachel mocked.

He pulled out a bottle of champagne. 'And I don't know how good this is, but I assume you like champers.'

'Indeed I do.'

She noticed his clothes. Chinos and a casual jacket and shirt.

'You're a bit well dressed for a picnic.'

'Oh, yes,' he replied as he popped open the champagne and poured two glasses. 'I've just had a sign-off meeting with my client. It means I've finished. I'm free until my train tomorrow.'

'Very nice.'

'Yes. Very beautiful.'

He handed her a glass.

'A toast,' he said. 'To random picnics with beautiful, smart, entertaining women.'

He stared deeply into her eyes as they chinked glasses and drank. The liquid warmed Rachel and his blue eyes seemed to pierce into her very core. He seemed so assured. He must do this sort of thing all the time, Rachel thought. She considered fleeing, before things went any further. But then where would she flee too? Back to an empty apartment? And besides, he was breathtakingly handsome. So instead of escaping, she took another sip of champagne, took a deep breath and turned to him.

She lifted her mouth to his and they kissed, tentatively at first, but then more passionately. His lips were soft and full and she gasped as she felt his tongue enter her mouth. She ran her fingers through his rich dark hair and he pulled her into his arms. She could feel him stroking her taut stomach muscles. Then he had her breast in his hand. His breathing became heavier, as did hers, as he squeezed her nipple. She felt the passion rising in her. What on earth was she doing? This was not Tom. This was not her husband. Oliver was a stranger. She pulled away from him. Oliver stroked her chin. 'I'm sorry,' he said. 'I… I got carried away. We'll stop.'

He moved away from her and in that instant,

Rachel realised she didn't care that she hardly knew this man. He was beautiful and he wanted her and she wanted him. She was suddenly in a D.H. Lawrence novel. Her life would be more complete after this moment. So she pulled him back to her.

'No, it's okay,' she whispered, huskily,

She reached out to cup his manhood through the fabric of his trousers and she could feel it bulging with anticipation. She rubbed and squeezed him, but he moved her hand away.

'Wait a minute,' he gasped. He stared at her with those deep blue eyes. 'Do you... should we... go back there?' He nodded his head in the direction of the secluded trees.

'Oh – yes.' Rachel felt she was losing all control.

He stood and swept her up and carried her into the wood. A few yards in they could no longer see the track. He kissed her and pushed her gently against a tree. With one hand he undid her bra and freed her breasts. He moved his mouth down, kissing her neck and then licking and kissing first one breast, then the other. He gently nibbled each nipple and Rachel thought she might faint with the pure pleasure. He ran his tongue over her stomach and sank to his knees in front of her. He lifted her skirt and began to kiss her through her silken knickers. Rachel held his head with both hands and pulled him into her. He deftly slipped her knickers down, then eased a finger into her dampness and buried his tongue inside her, nibbling and sucking her clitoris. Rachel gasped with pleasure and pressed her head back against the smooth trunk of the tree. She could feel the warm sun on her face as he worked her harder and harder until suddenly she could take no more and with a muffled scream she shuddered and came. She savoured the moment, then pulled away and knelt in front of him. She kissed him and slipped her hand inside his boxers. She gasped slightly despite herself as she pulled out his huge manhood and took it into her mouth, gingerly at first but ever more eagerly. Within a few short but strong strokes he was ready to explode after all the heightening tension, and, groaning, he twitched and came with a powerful shudder into her mouth. She held him in her mouth until the storm in his loins was over.

'Amazing.' Oliver smiled eventually. 'Who would have thought an innocent bike ride could bring such pleasures.' They both burst into laughter but stopped in shocked complicity when they heard voices from the track.

'Look,' said Oliver. 'Let's go back to my hotel. We can finish the picnic there or… well, whatever you fancy.'

Rachel knew exactly what she fancied. They arrived back at the hotel and went straight to Oliver's room. He stripped her slowly and laid her on the bed. She was amazed at how much she was enjoying this experience. And how free of guilt she felt. But she thought she might tell Oliver about Tom.

'I'm naughty, you know,' began Rachel. 'I'm not on my own. I'm...'

'Naughty, are you now?' interrupted Oliver as he slipped off his shirt and shorts and stood over her.

'Then turn over. You need punishing.'

'Yes, I do,' she smiled and rolled onto her stomach.

Oliver stroked her bottom, and then brought his hand down with a stinging smack. Rachel gasped as the sharp pain warmed her with pleasure. Tom slapped her again and spread her legs. He penetrated her with his finger and slapped again. Manipulating her with one hand and slapping with the other. Two, three times. Her rear was glowing red. Rachel could stand it no more. She wanted to scream with passion.

'Oh God, just fuck me!'

She rolled over and guided his heavy member toward her. He thrust roughly and buried himself completely inside her. She gasped with pure pleasure. 'Fuck me hard!'

They were like animals. She clawed his back and buttocks and bucked under him until, with a roar, he came again.

Rachel felt reckless and without care. She knew

Tom would not be back until late in the evening. This time was hers and Oliver would be gone forever tomorrow.

They played out Rachel's fantasies all afternoon. In the shower they came together. Back on the bed, he loosely tied her wrists and ankles and ravished her slowly. He even phoned a massage parlour and the very attractive brunette who turned up was more than willing to massage Rachel to orgasm while Oliver looked on, erect and ready to join in.

Eventually, however, it had to end. At eight o'clock they walked down to the hotel foyer together.

'You are very beautiful, Connie.' said Oliver, and kissed her. He stepped into the lift. 'Take care.'

'I will,' she said. And then, suddenly 'Of course, my name's not Constance. Sorry...'

As the lift door slid shut, he smiled. 'And my name's not Oliver. But I'll be back to review my project.' Then he was gone.

Rachel stood for a moment looking at the closed door. Not Oliver? It somehow didn't seem to matter. And would he ever find her again? Who knows, she thought. But what a difference a day makes. She turned on her heel on the polished marble floor and headed out into the balmy evening, back to her apartment and real life. And back to her husband. Who, she would insist, must buy a bike.

Acknowledgements

Thanks to
all our collaborators.

Other books in the series:

Agent Provocateur Secrets

ISBN 1-86205-720-6

Further reading:

Agent Provocateur Exhibitionist

ISBN 1-86205-714-1

www.agentprovocateur.com